D1637062

YO,
POE

YO, POE

FRANK
GANNON

VIKING

VIKING
Viking Penguin Inc., 40 West 23rd Street,
New York, New York 10010, U.S.A.
Penguin Books Ltd, Harmondsworth,
Middlesex, England
Penguin Books Australia Ltd, Ringwood,
Victoria, Australia
Penguin Books Canada Limited, 2801 John Street,
Markham, Ontario, Canada L3R 1B4
Penguin Books (N.Z.) Ltd, 182–190 Wairau Road,
Auckland 10, New Zealand

First published in 1987 by Viking Penguin Inc.
Published simultaneously in Canada

"A Terrible Saga of Entrées," "A Portrait of the Artist as a Young
Californian," "Yo, Poe," "The Price You Gotta Pay," "My New Season,"
and "Her Way" first appeared in *The New Yorker;* "Hamlet and
South Jersey" in *Philadelphia Magazine;* "The Southern Mind" and
"Kudzu East and West and South" (originally "Kudzu and the
Eastern Mind") in *Southern* magazine; and "What He Told Me" in
Gentleman's Quarterly.

LIBRARY OF CONGRESS CATALOGING IN PUBLICATION DATA
Gannon, Frank.
Yo, Poe.
I. Title.
PN6162.G32   1987   814'.54   86-40429
ISBN 0-670-81481-4

Printed in the United States of America by
The Book Press, Brattleboro, Vermont
Set in Garamond No. 3
Designed by The Sarabande Press

To Paulette

*I want to thank Kris Dahl, Jim Morgan,
Gerry Howard,
and especially Roger Angell.*

Contents

———

I Know What I'm Doing
About All the Attention I've Been Getting

1

A Terrible Saga of Entrées

5

Hamlet and South Jersey

11

Her Way

17

Riding the Trail of Many Tolls

21

A Portrait of the Artist
as a Young Californian

27

The Southern Mind

31

Daddy His Highness

35

Mass Mailing
41

Allegory of the Den in the Mail
47

Yo, Poe
51

Picasso's Men
55

In the Moors for the Season
61

Southern Living: One Man's Story
67

The Defense Rests
71

What the Russians Did to My Book
75

The Price You Gotta Pay
79

John Stern: American Man
85

Pretext for a Gathering
89

Kudzu East and West and South
95

Aspects of the TV Show
99

The Nevada Gaming Commission
Great Books Program
105

What He Told Me
113

Chitown Fans Bid Farewell to Hef
119

My New Season
123

YO,
POE

I Know What I'm Doing About All the Attention I've Been Getting

I was really worried about what to wear. It was like an anvil on my brain, just beating and beating and never stopping. Earlier that afternoon I saw someone walk into a clothes store and come out with a package. I knew what was in that package.

NEW CLOTHES.

It was like, Somebody bought some clothes, why can't I have some clothes too?

I went into my closet and got down on all fours and started to breathe really heavy. I was *trying* not to get nervous. I nudged a pair of brogans with my nose. Why not wear everything that's fallen off the hangers? It was a desperate, Hans Arp type of gesture, but what was left me? Yesterday I went to buy dog food in absolutely the worst thing: green shorts, gray socks, white sneakers. A brown shirt with the numeral "16" on the back. As soon as I walked into the grocery store I knew right away: wrong, *wrong,* WRONG!

But what could I do? It was too late then. I was trapped. I went through with it, but when I got to my car my heart was pounding and my face was flushed. My throat was dry and my hair was wet. My feet were bent and my back was twitchin'.

I'll *never* do that again.

I'm a quirky dresser. I'm absolutely fearless about what it is that I believe in. My shirts are incognizant and my socks—you must be completely *unaware* of my socks, that's, like, my approach to socks. My pants can be wily or even dishonest on some days if I just get up and feel that. But I have to feel it. When I wear a tie—and believe me, sometimes I really *wear* a tie—it can be porcine, straitlaced, odious. I have a certain little-boy quality, but there's also that big-fat-sweaty-guy thing in there too.

I've stopped taking myself so seriously. I can take a step back and laugh at myself. Sometimes I can get a really big charge out of what an absolute idiot I am. I'll have this big intellectual stumbling block right in my way, and suddenly I'll realize, Hey, who put the damn stumbling block there in the first place? That's right: Mister Serious Artist Person!

Whoa, I just crack up when that happens. Actually I'm a real easy laugher. I'll laugh at anybody who's being phony or pretentious. I'll laugh at anybody who's trying to make it the best they knew how. I'll laugh at anybody. Before I started getting all this attention, I was completely invisible. I could go where I wished and do what I liked without fear of being seen because I was completely invisible. I'm not making this up or being metaphorical here. I have the power to just completely turn off whatever it is in human beings that causes us to reflect light on the visible spectrum. So some nights I just make myself completely invisible and go for a walk. It's just this *power* I have. It's not like it was my life's dream or anything.

Anyway, people seem impressed by it. People would come up to me at parties and ask me about it. It made my girlfriend so mad. It was like she was really jealous or something. She finally told me that I had to choose between her and my ability to turn off whatever it is that causes human bodies to reflect visible light. That pretty well did in the relationship.

We still lived together, but it was like I was a sterilized needle and she was a little sliver of wood stuck in your finger. We could both tell what was going to happen so we decided to end it.

Now I'm in a whole new place. That other, older part of my life seems like some sort of surrealist joke that a bunch of my old buddies got together and pulled on me. Like they all got behind the furniture and waited until they heard me drive up, then they all jumped out and hit me with that part of my life.

But now I have to deal with now. I need some help on my clothes, so I just go manic and call everybody I can think of. They give me a lot of advice, but ultimately I'm the person under the hammer. It is I who have to wear the clothes, not all these well-wishers and hangers-on. Not the current artist of the month. Not all these vapid, air-brained media types. It will be me putting on the pants. It will be me pulling up the socks. I know how to do this. I've been at it for quite a while. I dressed myself for a long time before anybody was paying attention, and I'll dress myself a long time after everybody's paying attention to the way somebody else dresses himself. I know how these things go.

So what do I do? First I admit that I don't know what to do. Then I tell myself that I'm not alone, nobody else knows what to do either.

Once I've got that out of the way, I can start.

First I get out a big baggy pair of boxer underwear that is sort of right on the line between a lime and a grassy green. Then I go with the socks. They're white, but get this: they have this really thick black ribbing about an inch down from the top. Then I go with some gray trousers that really don't have anything to say, but I know that and that's what I want. Then I can tell that it's time for a black T-shirt. Don't ask me why, that's just the way I'm feeling. I put on some white sneakers, tie them quickly, and walk right out the door without a second thought.

That night I mingled. Everything went well because everybody was thinking that I had *planned* to look that way all along.

There's nothing permanent about this. I know that now. Tomorrow I'll be faced with more problems, but they won't be today's problems, they'll be newer, different problems. I can deal with it. I know what I'm doing.

A Terrible Saga of Entrées

Like the Mafia before them, Hell's Angels have begun to diversify into quasi-legal businesses. The FBI claims that neo-yuppie bikers have even started a catering service.

—*Newsweek*

It's early in the morning here in Washington and there's nobody on the streets but bums, cops, paper trucks, and caterers. Outlaw caterers from the bad end, menace living in their eyes, down and loud and screaming but not opening their mouths when they talk. Giving some kicks to the squares. Kicks like:

COQUILLES D'HOMARD MONBLASON
(for eight)
One hundred and ninety dollars

•

BAR FARCI
(for sixteen)
Two hundred and eighty-one dollars

5

•

These righteous dudes, they sure could sauté. They were a paradox. After I started to do business with them I always wondered how someone who knew where to find absolutely the best truffle in the Langhe in Piedmont could also be the kind of person to throw his mama on the back of an Electra Glide hog and ride off into whatever gastronomic thing waits out there in the night. I mean:

QUICHE LORRAINE
(for twenty-four)
Two hundred and ten dollars

•

QUICHE AUX FRUITS DE MER
(for thirty-six *avec* twenty-four mamas)
Four thousand dollars

•

ESCARGOTS EN COQUILLES
NUIT DE FAMILLE
(for fifty, *avec* about two hundred mamas)
Three million dollars

•

Yeah, these dudes could stick it. They could know it. They were into everything, and they were here.

•   •   •

We had them over to do the reception for the new Patagonian envoy. We were on the spot. Our chef here at the embassy had come apart during the Dinner Dance for the House Foreign Affairs Committee (with wives and staff), and we'd been waiting for weeks for his replacement from back home. We hadn't had much luck filling in with Deli Bungalow or the Rent-a-Burro Fiesta people. We were deep in the Yellow Pages, with the big holiday social season just ahead, and when we saw how things stood we called them.

Two of them came over just after midnight. They leaned their bikes at the foot of the marble steps and pushed their way in. I thought of Brando. They said they were booked up for ten months ahead but maybe they could handle our order if everything would go just as I described it.

"No problem," I said.

"No women in slacks, now," one said.

I didn't say anything. Our eyes met. We all knew where we were coming from.

They revved out of the embassy around two, throwing up the driveway gravel but generally taking it very easy as they cruised out past the guardhouses and headed up north, somewhere past Kalorama, to where there would be a whole lot of people like them: people shouting, drinking beer, and painting each other, people who had spent a great deal of time snail-watching on a farm in the South of France.

I understood them. We're into the cultural matrix here in D.C., and it's okay that *haute cuisine française* comes to you under certain conditions: tight leather jeans, studded kidney belts, wire-rim shades, arm tattoos, mild-fed veal, and get out of my face. You mess with these dudes and you've bought nothing but trouble—lumpy béarnaise, hollandaise that curdles nine times when you stir it, and your windows blown out with chocolate mousse.

It was all happening in the striped tents at nine in the evening. They'd told us that Sonny the Chef wouldn't make it, because he was still doing hard time for using Philadelphia Brand cream cheese in a Camembert gig. But Little Tommy would be there. At twenty-seven, he was already a leader—cold-eyed and clean-shaven, with a romaine-green Harley, and he'd given as good as he got in legendary rumbles with the Diablos, the heat, and Julia Child.

Everything looked good. The night was mild, the lanterns were shining, and our assistant attachés knew which senators' wives liked to waltz and which did the moon walk. Little Tommy wheeled in with the food—and then here came the Highway Patrol and it all turned into one big vapor lock. The pigs wrote up the boys for everything in the book: tomato skins in the Aubergine Caviar, grape seeds in the Caille en Aspic Muscat, no *pommes de terre* in the Pommes de Terre Biuchant. They also nailed them for seven blown mufflers. One biker said to me, "Tell your people back home that here in America, with all this abundance of great carbohydrates, you still get hassled by the pigs."

I've learned my lesson. No matter how tight you think you are with caterers, you always have to remember that you are not one of them. Despite their arm napkins, they can turn on you at any second. Later that evening, one of them caught a freshman representative (D., N.J.) putting ketchup on his Poire Belle Hélène, and the party was *finito*. In a minute, I was surrounded by a half dozen of the biggest, hairiest dudes in the history of French cooking. They called me a provincial, a philistine, and a water-drinker. Benno, the pastry chef—a paring-knife fight had taken off half his nose—burst into tears and told me the next time we had a sit-down affair we could just call the Colonel. A bad scene.

They got on their hogs and split. I watched them tear off—sixteen caterers in two rows, each with an emblazoned FÊTE ACCOMPLI on the back of his leather storm jacket—and privately I wished them well, for they were artists, after all. And they'd let us off lightly: $162,875.25, including tax and gratuities.

Hamlet
and
South Jersey

Shakespeare's *Hamlet* is superposed upon much cruder
material which persists even in the final form.

—T. S. Eliot

Years ago, when I was at Oxford, I developed a belief
in one single, universal human nature. I felt that all
human beings respond in a similar way to great art. The
plots, conflicts, and motivations in the major tragedies,
for instance, would always be clear, despite the cultural
diversity of the audience.

This theory remained for a long time just that—a
theory. Recently, though, I had the opportunity to test
it. This came about when I discussed the plot of *Hamlet*
with some inhabitants of a culture more primitive than
our own. I am speaking of the culture of South Jersey.

It was my second field trip to New Jersey, and after
some preliminary checking around, I decided to discuss
Shakespeare's great tragedy with one Nick Rotundo,

head of a household of ten, including, as Rotundo put it, his "no-good brother-in-law."

In South Jersey, the time between Memorial Day and Labor Day is spent near the ocean—an area referred to exclusively as "the shore." During this time of year, the inhabitants characteristically sit or lie motionless and imbibe the native beverage—what they call Schmidt's—and engage in the ritualistic "catching of rays."

Having little tolerance for these activities, I decided that this was an opportune moment to test my theory about the universality of human nature. In front of me sat the aforementioned Rotundo and two other elders: Frankie Croce, cutter of cold cuts, and Eddie Constantine, fitter of pipes.

We sat on the beach. Although I was no storyteller, I began to tell the story of Hamlet in the usual style.

"Long ago a thing occurred."

"What's 'occurred' mean?" asked Rotundo.

"Happened."

"Then say that," said Rotundo.

I apologized for being obscure and began again.

"Long ago a thing happened. One night, three men were keeping watch."

"Were they married?" asked Constantine.

"I don't know," I said. "I guess so."

"So they were chasin' tail," offered Croce.

"No," I said. "They were out on watch."

At this they all laughed.

"Watching for a little bit of this." Rotundo made a sort of punching motion with his right fist, and the three elders laughed again, heartily.

Slightly put off by this esoteric gesture, I began again.

"The three men see the dead king approach them, and he talks to them, or at least he gestures to them."

At this they were all taken aback, and they suggested that perhaps the king was not really dead, merely "really hung over."

Having no comment on this, I continued my narrative.

"The three men go and get the dead king's son. Then the king tells his son that his uncle, the dead king's brother, murdered the dead king. Then the murderer married the dead king's wife, the son's mother."

"What business was the old man in ?" asked Croce.

"He was a Danish king."

"Oh, like Entenmann's," offered Rotundo. "I get it. Go ahead."

"So when the son hears about what happened to his father, he is very upset, and he thinks about killing his uncle for revenge."

"Good idea," said Constantine, "but he should get somebody to do it for him, so he keeps his hands clean. With a big family business like that, I bet he could afford it easy."

"Yeah," said Croce. "What did you say they owned? Tastykakes?"

"Yeah," said Rotundo.

I went on.

"Hamlet, the son, is in love with Polonius's daughter, and when Hamlet starts acting odd because he's upset over what the ghost told him, Polonius tells Hamlet's uncle that Hamlet is acting odd because he's insanely in love with Polonius's daughter."

"He's acting odd?" said Croce. "*I'll* give him acting odd."

I chose to ignore this.

"Polonius tries to eavesdrop on Hamlet because Polonius wants to know what Hamlet has planned. But Hamlet stabs Polonius and kills him."

This brought many comments.

"What a creep."

"Sleazebag move."

"Acting odd? *I'll* give him odd."

"Gimme a brewski."

I hurried to complete my story.

"Polonius's son, Laertes, has a sword fight with Hamlet, but little does Hamlet know that Laertes's sword has poison on it. Also, Hamlet's uncle has a cup of—" I looked around. "He has a cup of poisoned brew. And he's going to give it to Hamlet to drink, just in case Laertes doesn't get a chance to stab Hamlet with the poisoned sword."

"So what happened?" asked Rotundo.

"What happened was, Hamlet and Laertes switch swords in the fight after Hamlet has already been cut. Hamlet's mother drinks the poison by mistake. Hamlet kills Laertes, and then he goes over and kills his uncle. Then Hamlet dies because he's been stabbed earlier with the poison sword."

I stopped, relieved, and listened to the reactions of the elders.

"Pretty good," said Croce. "It's like, whaddayacallit? Survival of the fittest, right?"

"I like it," said Constantine. "We oughta get rid of all these bums on welfare."

"Hey, tell me about it," said Rotundo.

The sun was now setting, and the elders offered me

a brew, complimenting me on my story. They asked me to tell them other stories, but not just then because the Phils were on the tube.

Thus I learned from the inhabitants of South Jersey that all great art is universal, and our response to it, despite the diversity of human culture, is the same the whole world over.

Her Way

We all knew Kitty. She was always asking you questions. Everybody was used to seeing her family's name in the phone book. In that same phone book were the names of many known criminals. A Mr. Ted Bundy appears. Al Capone is there. William Bonny, who had the same name as the infamous Billy the Kid, also appears.

"I remember Kitty tape-recording me all the time," says Don Johnson (not his real name). "Everybody knew Kitty. By the time she was twenty, she'd already tape-recorded everybody in the neighborhood twenty or thirty times."

Kitty was, right from the start, a leader. She organized the pep club at her high school, was active in her church, played the piano, and tripped up (Q.A. or some such?) farm animals.

"She was a very busy girl," said Ed (Too Short) Smith, a longtime friend of the family (not his real name). "She was the first person who ever told me to pour borax in my ear. She was always the person you would go to in emergencies."

Her parents understood how much tape-recording meant to her at an early age. Her father was a carpet installer and her mother was, at one time, one of the major interpreters of Thomas Holcroft and a damn good hand with anything hydraulic (not their real jobs).

"We gave her everything," they probably said. "We don't feel real great about the way she turned out, but that's none of our business. We're only her parents."

Yet she had that something, that something that you can't define or even recognize. Yet it was always there. That something. Finally somebody learned how to take advantage of that something. The man for the job turned out to be Magic Johnson (not his real name).

"I thought that if I could get Kitty to say nothing good about anybody for maybe three or four months, if we could just pack it all in like that, then we would really be after something," Magic said. "I knew that the mood of the country was just right for it."

In the early days, Kitty could only say bad things about people under twenty-five. In time, it became vital for her to be able to speak badly of everyone, no matter what the age. Almost immediately, as if by instinct, she amazed everyone by saying that Bernard Baruch liked to tongue-kiss. All over the country people picked up on this. There was someone new on the horizon, and this someone had *nothing* nice to say.

Her climb was meteoric. She became, overnight, a household word. Her work appeared in every major magazine and her books were read everywhere. She appeared on talk shows, news shows. She continued, however, to trip up (Q.A.) farm animals.

"Why not?" she might have said. "They're there aren't they?"

Then Kitty met Herman Melville, and everything

changed. (I'm pretty sure that's not his real name.) "Melville was tall, intense, bearded, aloof—everything Kitty was after," says a mutual friend. "Herman Melville became a kind of obsession with her. Melville was cruel to her, but then I guess you could say that Kitty was the same way toward him. They also both have really big lips, don't you think?"

Melville and Kitty. They chased each other over several continents. Once, after one of their infamous quarrels, Melville locked himself in a footlocker with some ricotta cheese and said not to bother him unless Kitty apologized. The next day they were all lovey-dovey, walking hand in hand to see an illegal pit-bull fight. It was all a game to them.

One night Kitty happened to pick up a copy of *Moby Dick*. She read the inscription:

"IN TOKEN OF MY ADMIRATION FOR HIS GENIUS, THIS BOOK IS INSCRIBED TO NATHANIEL HAWTHORNE."

"You could have fried an egg on her forehead when she saw that inscription," says a close friend, who didn't want me to refer to him by any name. "I tried to explain the big mistake she was making, but it was no use. I told her that Melville and Natty Hawthorne went way back together. Everybody knows that the two of them and Bronson (Lips) Alcott played in the same sax section for Kay Kyser (not his real name, but close). (Q.A.) She just wouldn't listen to reason when she got in one of her moods. She was almost suicidal. The next day, though, I'd see her and Melville like a couple of lovebirds, tampering with some Tylenol packages."

Of course, Kitty and Melville were never meant to be. After "the Herman thing," as her friends called it, Kitty fell into many arms—and of course she screamed.

Someone who claims to have known Kitty says, "She has her problems. Who doesn't? But all in all she's a kind and loving person, and a wonderful tape-recorder operator, and a terrific person who wouldn't think twice about misquoting anybody who got in her way."

Riding
the Trail
of Many Tolls

"Cowboy capitalism" has hit the financial markets.
—*Newsweek*

We rode in a limo,
Me and my associate, Mort;
I made one call on the way
And I sold something short.
—*Old trail song*

We came up the Jersey Turnpike the summer of '84.
We bunked down at the Marriott Essex House. We
washed our faces and cleaned our guns and scratched
ourselves and checked our coats. Then we ordered room
service.

Or, I should say, *some* of us ordered room service.
The steel-tempered among us did not.

We were the bold men in gray and blue with Windsor
knots and half-Windsor knots. We were the ones who
moved the paper, fighting taxis and construction and
detours and each other and whatever in hell else God

made. We rode to our leveraged buyout knowing full well in our hearts that when we were gone there'd be no song of glory, no parades, no monuments, and no pretty girls to remember us. Just a sad-eyed staff attorney and some empty seats in an expense-account bar.

We rode the long miles to where the buildings rise to the big blue sky, riding a day's work for a day's tax-sheltered gain. We rode as one, but we weren't as one. Some of us still clung to the old ways, the old cowboy ways. And the old cowboy songs. We sat in the back of the limo and sang the old songs. We sang with the voices of the sons of the pioneers.

One wild soul we called "Houston" sat there and called Houston. When he got Houston he crooned "The Streets of Laredo" into the phone. The man who heard that song was a square, powerful man with a set jaw. There was no give in that man. "No more give than a rock in the desert gives," I heard his wife say once. He was a man they called "CPA."

This wasn't my first day doing this and it won't be my last, unless some sidewinder gets the jump on me. I've been on the trail a long time, and I guess I know this trail as good as any.

I guess I've spent half my life looking at life between a horse's ears. That's just what I was doing today, too. Then somebody told me to put the horse's ears down because it was an object d'art.

Things like that just roll off my back. Keep goin', is what I always say.

Then we heard that sound. Jay Crenshaw. Singin' that song. That song he always sung. He always sat in the back of the limo and he always sang that song. Lord, how he loved that song! We would put up with his singing (which we hated) just because we knew how much he loved that song.

> I hope when I'm gone
> And the Dow stays the same
> You'll hear the headwaiter
> Just calling my name.
>
> Then I'll look down
> From heaven above
> Between those horse's ears
> But filled up with love.
>
> I'll pity my partners,
> I'll be so much wiser,
> I'll even look down
> On Louis Rukeyser.

There was always a stillness when he finished.

It was an old, old song. A trail song. It was the same song his daddy had taught him on the long trail to boarding school. When Crenshaw had a son, he would teach it to him. Or at least mail him a copy.

Before us lay the Hudson. We were corporate raiders and we knew our work. We knew that there might be trouble. When you've been in as many proxy fights as I have, and been in as many struggles for director's seats as I have—well, you know at least this: you're no stranger to trouble. You've seen it all. Junk bonds. Arbitrageurs. You've even buried your best friend after a bad wave of shareholder protest.

Still, you didn't go looking for trouble. Trouble would

23

find you soon enough. Either find you, or have you paged.

I never knew why I took the course I did. More than likely, it was simply the love of wild country and wild life. All for its own sake. I could never see the tame way. That's why, once in a while, I wore loafers with a business suit. Don't ask me why. I couldn't tell you if I knew.

In the morning we stormed downstairs, fourteen strong. Fourteen strong. Shoulder to shoulder. Looking one way. Heads in a row. Heads down. Eyes up. Fourteen head. Fourteen strong. Fourteen guys.

Getting on the elevator.

Fourteen. Fourteen stong to the damn hitching post. From the rough country. Weathered and beaten and strong in the broken places.

Fourteen. From New Jersey.

They knew the asparagus spears. And the Garden State Parkway and the Garden State Track. And they knew the Meadowlands and the shore. They knew how the shore was, and they knew how the shore wasn't.

They also knew some Comanches.

We had come up the turnpike with thirty thousand preferred shares. It was late in the day and the exhaust fumes were thick, but the tolls were the same. And we rode tough and we were used to it by now. Used to the grit and the soot.

Used to the trail.

.   .   .

Fourteen strong, wide as a spreadsheet (a real spread-sheet, not one of those computer things). Heading out. Head down, eyes up. Missing nothing and nothing missing us. Our jaws set stubbornly. This was because we had brought many herds through rough country. (We will not confirm that in writing, however.)

Going now. Moving now. Going and moving to see James T. Anderson II.

James T. Anderson II was a narrow weasel man. A dry-as-dust man. A pay-as-you-go man. A wear-glasses-and-maybe-be-your-client man. His eyes were milky. His cheeks were hollow. When he talked it was like the wind through the scrubs. He started to talk, and for a moment I wondered why I heard the wind rustling through what sounded like outside vegetation.

Then I figured it out. I caught on. I was just a ramrod, but I catch on. The trail gives as it takes.

Anderson wanted to tell us that he had revised his offer. Downward.

I looked out the window. The sun was disappearing into the horizon, just as I had seen it do so many times before.

Soon the coyotes would be calling. Probably collect.

A Portrait
of the Artist
as a Young
Californian

Once upon a time, and a very good time it was, there
was a little boy named George who wanted to learn how
to read and speak three languages before he was five
and learn how to play the piano and the violin and tennis,
and he also wanted to become literate at the computer
and learn how to eat a lot of roughage and exercise
sensibly and experience excellence.

His father told him that story. His father had a very
good and lasting tan.

He was little George. And he was the one in the
story. He was the one who experienced excellence.

He knew that song. It was his song.

> Suzuki violin and French lessons at three
> What a nicens little baby this Georgie
> will be.

Daddy was older than Mommy. Mommy has changed her face three times and she will keep doing that because she wants to be the best me that she can.

> Tra la la lala
> Tra la la lala
> Flatten your stomach.

It was very important to have a flat stomach. It made you a much better me.

I was feeling bogus. I was mega, but not mega enough for the job. And I was a little amped if you want to know the truth because a little earlier I was probably a pooh pirate, and I'm not. I'm a breeder, nothing but. I'm not steadfast, but show me a tight little unit and I'll shred her.

So when I was first a product of a relationship, I was imposing right from the first go. I mean when I was a wee squid it was Biafra and I had to crash with my little sister, but that was cool. I got to scope out babes without getting haired. So tell me I'm a zisker and I'll tell you you're in the soapbox derby for whales.

My sister if you must know is as gnarly as they come. That bwana was fresh. Munga. I'm not a reknob and I know the program. I jam on the taboos, but my sister was rad. Thrashmatic. So we're in the same rack and I figure she's going to say the whole prono pups just totally grikes, but I'm not far along in the program and I can still remember my tail.

So I'm thinking I'm either going to throw darts at this unit or get chinese-eyed. I scope right away that she does not groove on the Arthropoda, and she hairs in their presence. She would not be freaked by the Mexican Air Force, but she spins out at the sight of the little furry ones.

So right away I figure that it's got to be jam and tripendicular to groove with the eight-armers. I do not pretend to understand this mega-aversion that she is harboring, but I've got some confid working and pretty soon the whole thing scopes out fully munga.

I'm not grain-fed, but I know a gomer and they always have their theme. They act like a gork for weird on the moving mall stairs. Or they blow a hype on the pigeon tower. Or they go sckacks when they see carbos and run in to worship the portentous Buick. I have been around the track, even as a squid. I have dropped the bomb. When things got gay I have always opted to shine. I know when Big Ben says to book. I know when to voice over, and I know which sluts have been burgered out. I've been from ritual to romance and I grokked all the input you have, and probably more.

Still, I'm aggro over this momma who is my sister in my rack in the slurbs. I don't want to sound raspy, but it is very sketchy between the rayon in that lair. If you can't buy it, iron a prune. So my head is airmailed to New Jersey because I'm constantly gumming out over this incubus. Urr to the quantum level.

Like my progenitor says, I needed arresting. But I needed a wheeze in the worst of all possible worlds. I went for it, and I don't mind telling you, even though you probably think I am poor protoplasm.

Be hard-core. See what falls out of the tree on you. Don't take it to dinner. You may be asked to move away from the normals. You may have to take a three-and-a-half and go back to the primordial soup and the heshers.

I came with the little furry ones and it was a wheeze among the wheezes on Olympus and the birds stopped singing so they could scope it out. We have on these diapers. The white breechcloth for those who have newly aspired. Byzantine, these words they have for everything.

I got a spanking. For scaring my sister with a spider. Totally sixties.

The Southern Mind

———◆———

I am hurtin'. When you look at me you see HURT like the letters in BEN HUR with the chariots driving underneath the H.

I am an ANGRY man. I am a SICK man. I am an ANGRY, HURT, and SICK man. It's been like that for a long time.

Still. You think I'm going to walk around like that, with my head hunched between my shoulders, walk through the city streets that have no pity? I don't even like the city streets.

What I will do is, I will just sit here for a while. Maybe twenty minutes. Then I will do what I have to do. And what I have to do is find a symbolic way of expressing myself.

Once I find that, all bets are off.

We are in a drought condition here where I live. Four weeks ago it just quit raining, and that was it. Just quit. Shut off. No water.

31

So this boy who lives behind me just won't leave his sprinkler alone. He won't turn it off. Even at night, you're ready to go to sleep and what do you hear?

Chi . . . chi . . . chi . . . chi . . . chi . . .

I feel guilty flushing the damn toilet and this boy is running his water sprinkler at night.

That's the situation, but do I do anything?

I do something.

We have here a little newspaper called the *Tri-County Shopping News*. In the back of this paper there is a section called "Tell Your Neighbor Ads." This week, one of them near the middle says: HEY, NEIGHBOR. THIS IS A DROUGHT. TURN OFF THE DAMN SPRINKLER. NEIGHBOR.

When I saw that paper I thought, *Good damn symbolic protest.*

It wasn't my first symbolic protest. I've been into it for a long time. Sometimes I think that symbolic protest is my life's work.

I need to let everybody know how I feel, but I don't feel like telling them. We Southerners are always looking for the *gesture.* That's because we're *very* literal-minded. No smoky, half-buried meanings for us. Give me a damn symbol. If you don't like me, shoot my dog. Please! Then I will know.

Let's get it out of the way. Or don't shoot my dog. Same thing.

When I was about to be married I went out and bought wedding rings. I was driving home and I saw some boys I knew. We got in a football game. We had a lot of fun.

When I got home, though, I looked in my pocket and there was nothing in there.

I had lost the rings, the wedding rings, playing football with my buddies. I was very irritated, but I thought I could get over it.

Then I realized the truth.

I would never "get over it."

I had engaged in my first symbolic protest.

On that day my life began. It's a life I now take pride in. The simple, basic life of symbolic protest.

Of course, what we can't escape facing in all of this is the big thing: Everything is symbolic. If you walk into a bait shop and you don't have a hat on, I bet you nobody asks you anything friendly about bream. Nobody will ask you how your mommanem is. Nobody will even look at you. Go into a bait shop without a hat and you might as well be in a shopping mall.

No one denies the power of symbols. This tangled Southern wood is filled with them.

Daddy
His Highness

by
Elizabeth Tudor

———————◆———————

Chapter One

England in the 1500s was already a country of legends
and past history. In those days monarchs built castles
and lived in them. Armor-clad knights roamed the coun-
tryside in search of what were called "jousting matches."
It was an income-tax-free Utopia, as one of Daddy's
friends termed it. Yet throughout the land, one figure
united these multifarious people: Henry Tudor, the king,
my dad.

Our house was a vast place, befitting our standard of
living. There were hundreds of guards and servants.
There was also one little funny man whose only purpose
seemed to be to bring me laughter in my life. I loved
him very much, but I can't remember his name. Even
now, I remember him only as "the jester."

The smart people were as happy as they had ever
been when Daddy became king. Daddy was not the

stupid man that many people said he was. He loved dancing and masquerades, but he also loved art, serious literature, and beheadings. I remember one courtier saying about Daddy, "He's a lot smarter than a lot of the bozos we've had around here." Daddy was, too. He was no dummy.

Daddy valued a sense of humor, and he encouraged us to develop one. He loved dirty jokes—both hearing and telling. I used to try to leave the room when he was engaged in one of his sessions with Wolsey, but I always tried to be secretive about it. Daddy did not like it if you did not appreciate his smutty jokes about Martin Luther.

I've often wondered about a lot of things concerning Daddy and me. If he had treated me differently, would English history have been different? Would the government have become secularized and weakened? Would the people have tolerated being led from an infallible pope to an even more self-aggrandized monarch? And, most important, would Daddy have looked better without a beard?

When I was young, Daddy was faced with a lot of problems that were affecting his home life. One of his big problems was financial, although he always made a big deal about what a "good job" he had. He wanted to enlarge the navy and buy carpeting, and he was thinking about wallpaper. He found, though, that the coffers were empty. He also found that he didn't have any money.

It was during this time, in the summer, when an incident happened that burned its way painfully into my memory.

I was at home downstairs counting the candles. It was

one of my favorite ways of amusing myself. On nights like this, when he wasn't busy, Daddy and I would have dinner. Daddy always pretended it was like a "date," but I knew differently. Just as we were settling down to eat, some monarch or noble or other unwanted-by-me person would arrive, and I'd be left staring at my mutton while they discussed things like "papal intrusion" and "divers sundry things." They would never think of telling me—a mere child in their eyes—what "divers sundry" meant. They had their own specialized language, these "important" people, and someone like me could never hope to understand. I grew swiftly bored and went back to counting the candles.

Chapter Ten

Daddy had his rules. Sometimes he called them his "royal prerogative." He wrote them down one time, on a servant. There weren't that many rules—which was good for the servant, who was small.

As a punishment for breaking any of the rules, I had to clean Buckingham Palace, which was a big place with a lot of mirrors and some throw rugs.

Once, as a punishment for spilling pudding on a pair of Daddy's particolor underwear, I had to clean up Buckingham Palace *and* wind all the clocks. It took me all day, but when Big Ben, which was a clock, tolled at the end of the day, I was satisfied that I had done a good job. It was not, however, good enough for Daddy. I was sound asleep in my bed when he burst into my room and dragged me down the hall, down the steps, out the door, and over to—you guessed it—the Tower of London. Then he dragged me up the steps. Then he realized he was thinking of another building, and he dragged me down the steps. Then, just for the hell of it, he dragged me down some steps that he encountered on the way back home.

Oh, how I hate this stupid bastard, even if he is the king, I thought. But I did not say anything.

Then, when we were nearly home, I made a classic mistake. I said that I really didn't think I had done such a bad job of cleaning the palace and winding the clocks, even though I might have missed some corners. Then I added that papal infallibility sounded like a good deal to me. Daddy flew into a rage. Later, however, he returned through a window and beat me over the head with a stuffed woodchuck for an hour and a half.

Chapter Thirty

Jane Seymour was the first steady girlfriend Daddy had had since Mommy. Jane was happy and fun-loving, and I thought she was the prettiest woman I had ever seen. Jane was very good to me. On Boxing Day she always brought me a new pair of gloves, trunks, and headgear.

She had a silly sense of humor, yet I loved her.

I was very young when Daddy was going out with her, and I asked her once if she was going to be my new mommy. She just smiled and said, in that way she had, "Only if your father threatens to behead me."

I really liked Jane Seymour.

.   .   .

Today I try to think back to an objective way about Daddy and his life. Daddy was never very clear just what the situation at home had been when he was growing up, but I know that it was probably unpleasant. . . .

I used to think, once in a while, that Daddy actually might have wanted to have a boy instead of me. Later, however, I was able to dismiss such notions as paranoia on my part.

Today, though, I am able to deal with the situation and look anybody in the eye, except Francis Drake, who is too tall. I am a survivor.

Mass Mailing

Bhagwan Shree Rajneesh, the Indian guru deported
from the United States, expelled from Greece, and
barred from Britain, has been given an entry permit
for Ireland, the Justice Department said.
—*Associated Press,* March 15, 1986

BHAGWAN SHREE RAJNEESH

Love has come. To you. This letter that you hold
in your hands is made of love.

I have sent it. I am love.

I love your land. It is very nice here. I can see
why it is called the Emerald Isle. Emeralds are very
expensive gems, the most exquisite things I can
think of quickly.

May I take this opportunity to mention our little
group. We meet on a regular basis for discussions,
meals, encounters, and, yes, some bowling.

Enlightenment is achieved when consciousness
peaks.

Please take a moment to look at the enclosed
brochure.

BOARD OF TOURISM

Dear Mr. Rajneesh,

Thank you very much for your letter expressing an interest in Ireland.

Few travelers would argue that spring is Ireland's finest hour, so it's easy to see how even a man who calls himself the Swami of Sex might fall prey to the get-away-from-it-all syndrome and head for our smiling shores.

If I may speak for all of us, and I guess I can, I wish you and your "clan" a memorable time in the land of saints and scholars.

A little about us. We're a small island in the Atlantic about—oh, eighty miles away from another small island you might be more familiar with, England. We offer you an endless variety of ways to relax or, if you're up for it, have excitement day and night.

Friendly people, scenic beauty, and golf links abound. As a matter of fact, I bet you didn't know that Ireland has more golf courses per square mile than any other country in the world! So you'll be sure to find a course that becomes your own personal Buddhafield.

Whether it's shopping for the finest in clothing, linen, or glasswear or just, as you suggest, "surrounding yourself with a cadre of fanatics," you'll find it here in Ireland. And it's affordable.

Yours for enlightenment,
Andrew Forde
Board of Tourism

PS. I couldn't tell you what to do with all those cars. Bring 'em along and we'll do something. Parades?

EDITORIAL

This morning I find that I have received by post a number of papers inviting me to become a member of the loyal of the Rajneesh-puram and to pay a lot of my money to the people involved with this particular enterprise. They have invited me to their meetings, and they say that I will get to meet the Swami of Sex. There will also be a lot of "fun" and, if I could get rid of my mood of Homeric detachment and "surrender to it," I might achieve enlightenment. Also, they implied, if I could be seen in public sober for once in my life, I might dance right into a peak of consciousness and spend the rest of my days having annual dinners on the Buddhafield.

The program seems sound. To me. But I often spend a great deal of time among rascally non-brows that I am happy to number among the corps of my friends. Are you trusting me in this matter? Is this "Bog-wan" just another malcontent mailing out his envelopes, living in a world of menacing mumble, toying with the life-style of an extortionist, trafficking with illiterate sluts and parrot-clawed literary hippocritics?

These questions and more I will answer the day after tomorrow, or sooner.

Dear Bagwan Shree Rajneesh,

Thanks for your letter. I don't think you really wrote it, though. Still, I received it and held it in my hands while I read it. It was a fine letter, one of the best of its kind. Its *genre* was problematic. Subhuman scratchings? Fleshy ramblings?

No matter. A brave effort. Now that we're friends, I also have something I'd like to invite you in on. So crack the door and here's what.

I've been, as you know, going at the ponies for all of my life. I've lived at the same address for thirty-nine years, mailing out my insights to my friends and interested parties. In all this time there has been no keening on the part of anyone involved.

Behind? Why not jump on the train?

Fifteen a week for sixteen "dart-player" exactions from the pony herd. Once-in-a-long-age SPECIALS, which come up very seldomly, are available, when available, as STEAL THE MONEY DISCOUNT PLUCKS. Can't go wrong with these, as long as God keeps giving them to me.

The door is closing. The train is leaving. Down those tracks to fast animals and sensational gains.

Bagwan, my friend, the time is now. I have very few friends, but I count you as one of them.

God bless you.

> Yours in sensational winners,
> "Big Liam"
> THIRTY-NINE YEARS AT
> THE SAME ADDRESS

Dear Bhagwan Shree Rajneesh,

In the bog. One.

Yet may we see the hoo-rah aslumbered in the rolls with the vacant ninety-seven rolls, they sans old doe-eyes snoozing, all in-a-row.

You swami. The prize of your save is the price of my spend.

In the bog. One.

Anonymous

Allegory of the Den in the Mail

A work of High Culture is occasionally popular,
though this is increasingly rare.

>   —Dwight Macdonald,
>   "A Theory of Mass Culture"

Almost any situation in life can be classified as a "sales
situation."

>   —Robert J. Ringer,
>   *Winning Through Intimidation*

DISCOVER A UNIQUELY
AMERICAN WORLD OF ROMANCE
WITH MAJOR WORKS OF THE
WORLD'S PHILOSOPHERS

Only in America. . . .

MAJOR WORKS OF THE WORLD'S PHILOSOPHERS are
among the first works to explore today's new love relationships. These searing authors will open up new worlds
of sensuality and romance. Thrill to Augustine and his
shockingly frank *Confessions*. Climb to new heights of

pleasure with Roy Wood Sellars as he goes in quest of *Physical Realism*. And go beyond the G-spot and experience Aristotle's *Organon*!

These compelling major works of philosophy reach into the hearts of people across America, probing into the most intimate moments of romance, love, logical syntax, sex, desire, ethics, and today's new male-female relationships.

You'll follow beautiful heroines and virile heroes as they unflinchingly face today's most puzzling choices. Career first, marriage later? Trading sex for professional advancement? Acknowledging certain concepts as unanalyzable? "Giving in" to be popular? Denying causality? Lovers outside the traditional marriage structure. The rationalistic approach to nature. Teen sex. All that makes love what it is. It's all captured in the warm pages of these tender books.

JUST FOR YOU—ACT NOW AND
GET A SPECIAL OFFER

Now you can enter this world of sex, sensuality, and concepts understood in a figurative sense. Just return the enclosed card. You'll get five free works of philosophy specially selected from our popular series. And, if you write an *a posteriori* statement in the space provided, you'll also get a free copy of *Summa Contra Gentiles*, a book that dares to expose the theology and metaphysics of today's hot new singles!

ONLY ABOUT 12¢ A DAY!

If you decide to become a MAJOR WORKS OF THE WORLD'S PHILOSOPHERS at-home thinker, you'll automatically receive three monuments of mankind's search for truth each and every month. All you'll pay is an average of 12¢ a day. Think of it. For the price of a single shoelace you'll be entering into the spirit of philosophical inquiry and the spirit of today's changing male-female sex roles! That's all you pay! We pay everything else.

ACT NOW

Don't wait. Act now. Remember, Bergson said that it is inappropriate to limit thought to spatial concepts; time, in particular, should not be conceived of as extension. Join today's new, ever-changing male-female relationships!

THE MAJOR WORKS OF THE
WORLD'S PHILOSOPHERS'
GUARANTEE OF SATISFACTION

You must be completely satisfied with each work of philosophy that you receive. We mean 100 percent satisfied, too. We're not talking about partial satisfaction here, if you know what we mean! If at any time you are less than thrilled with the romance, sex, love, male-female relationships, principal ideas advanced, or the picture on the cover, just let us know and we'll stop sending you major works of philosophy just like that. How can we do it? How can we be so sure of ourselves? Simple. We've been publishing since Wittgenstein was knee-high. We know how people feel about philosophy.

USE THIS CARD TO ENTER A
UNIQUELY AMERICAN WORLD
OF BEING AND NOTHINGNESS

Find out what makes Americans so different when it comes to love and logical positivism. Send for your free MAJOR WORKS OF THE WORLD'S PHILOSOPHERS. There's no obligation, if you didn't read what we said earlier. Do it today!

Yes! Send me my works of philosophy. I want to be an at-home thinker. As such, I will receive many books that I will have to pay for. I understand that I'll be mailed these books automatically whether or not I want them. I also realize that the unexamined life is not worth living.

Yo, Poe

Consider [Sylvester Stallone's] pet project: a film bi-
ography of Edgar Allan Poe. "I am a student of his,"
says Stallone. "But people have this image of Poe as a
crazy alcoholic and drug addict, and that's wrong. I'd
like to set the record straight."   —*Newsweek*

It is with a lot of humility that I pen the first sentence
of this work. It is almost accompanied by a sense of
trembling awe that I approach the reader with this, the
most dreamlike, the most solemn, the most difficult, the
most buried-in-my-gut.

Hey, Ulalume, if I could sing and dance I wouldn't
have to do this.

O strangely sent one, how your words touch my spirit!
How well have we both learned the propensity of man
to define the indefinable! How the strange happiness of
our innermost souls has thus been magnified!

You really got lucky tonight, you know?

It's a quiet and still afternoon here. The leaves are all
sere, whatever that means. But here inside the Spectrum
it's a different story. Men are screaming, women are

51

fainting, and the children—well, they're just being kids.

Right you are, Al. There's tumult everywhere, and with good reason. I've never seen anything quite like it.

No, Dick, I haven't either. You can almost feel the electricity in this arena. It's almost palpable.

I can't keep up with you, Al.

I've been going back to school, Dick. Heh, heh.

Excuse me for interrupting, but here he comes.

Making his way down the aisle with his entourage— Mister Edgar Allan Poe.

Some say his last name is Allan, some say it's Poe. There's quite a bit of controversy about that, Al.

All I know is he looks serious tonight, Dick.

Look at those eyes. Look at that expression.

He means business.

Yes, he does, Al. And there's that tie.

That trademark Edgar Allan Poe tie. He's still wearing it, and I guess he always will, Dick.

You can bet on that, Al.

But no raven tonight, Dick.

You're not going to get me to say "Nevermore," Al.

Heh, heh. You know, a lot of people don't know that Edgar Allan Poe was actually a very good broad jumper.

That's right, Al. A lot of critics feel that he may have symbolically put himself in his famous story "Hop-Frog."

You're a regular encyclopedia, Dick.

Hello again, litetature fans. Tonight we have a special treat on our post-fight show. Tonight's guest is Baudelaire, the unofficial manager of Edgar Allan Poe.

Edgar Poe. I always call him Edgar Poe. Please don't

say "Edgar Allan Poe." I hate that. It makes me—how you say?—sick.

Okay, Beau, have it your way. Edgar Poe.

Gracias, amigo.

Let's get right to the big question. Why do you, the acknowledged champion of the symbolists, want to manage a guy like Poe, an alcoholic drug addict who marries little girls because he's a pervert? And on top of all that, he can't tie a tie.

Let me get this straight right away. And not just for you, Marv. For everybody. Edgar Poe is not a pervert. He is not an alcoholic. To my knowledge, the man has never taken a drink. He does not use drugs. He is not a "party" person.

How about the tie allegation?

I can't say anything about that. He's an individual, and like all individuals he has a right to his own tastes in neckwear.

You don't think he looks funny?

No. But let me say one thing.

Go right ahead.

My man was actually an excellent athlete.

You mean you're going to get into the broad-jumping thing and "Hop-Frog" and all of that?

Absolutely.

Good for you. And while we have you, you'll forgive another question, I'm sure. How is Rimbaud?

Loved it. I was on my feet cheering.

There you have it. Baudelaire, the self-styled king of the symbolist poets. Nothing if not controversial. Thank you for coming.

Gracias.

.   .   .

Virginia. Yo, Virginia—wake up. I have something I want to tell you. I was just over to look at the poster they got of me. And you know what? They got the wrong tie. That's right. They got me wearing a club tie instead of this little one that I always tie funny.

I just want to say a couple of things. One, a lotta people probably think it was kinda weird for me to get married to you, on account of you being my cousin and only fourteen years old and like that. What they don't know is that for a guy like me beauty is incarnate only as an intellectual principle. Man is but a part of the great will that pervades the cosmos. In other words, when I hear somebody say something about my wife I tell him to get out of the car.

I got one more thing I want to say. Some of my early biographers, they got the idea that I was an alcoholic drug addict or something. That's just a bunch of you know what. I'm not a drug addict, I'm a poet. Keats, Shelley—they were poets and they died young. But it wasn't because they were drug addicts. It was because they didn't train.

Tonight I'll know one thing. If I hear that rapping, that rapping on my chamber door, and I'm sitting there. Still sitting there, pondering over a big pile of quaint and curious volumes. If I'm still sitting there, I'll know one thing: the record is now straight.

Picasso's
Men

On the Parnassus that is modern art, one name occupies the place of honor: Pablo Picasso. More than anyone else in our century he shaped the very way we think about and experience the visual arts.

To study Picasso is, in the fullest sense, to study modern art. Picasso and modern art: the two are inseparable. If you study modern art and leave out Picasso, you probably took a course though the mail, but it's too late now. Try and get a refund. What are you going to do, sue the post office box number?

Maybe not, right?

Picasso. No one can leave him out. Everybody looks real good if they're talking about Picasso. The man was a genius. He was the greatest artist in the world. He's never left out of any survey course on modern art. It's almost impossible to overrate Picasso's importance.

You can't get a decent job without it.

More than anything else, Picasso had *eyes*. Both of his eyes worked, and he used them constantly, often independently, all day long. He saw things his way.

And his way was the way of modern art.

Picasso, as is well known, was greatly influenced in his art by the many women that walked in and out of his life. Aren't we all?

Too much has been written on this subject. No need to read any more about that. 'Nuff said.

But what about the influence of the man himself? Who in fact did Picasso influence?

In that strange, mirrorlike way that nature so often adopts, it turns out that Picasso had his biggest influence on *men*.

Influenced by women. Influencing men. Who can hope to explain the paradox that is art?

We can only look. And approve.

If Picasso attracted and influenced men, as it seems he must have, one thing is certain: it was not because of their looks. Among Picasso's "inner circle" there were many men, but they are a study in contrasts. Fernande Valdez, Picasso's mailman, is, in Valdez's own words, "an emaciated little prunelike man." Yet Picasso's garbageman, Marcel D'Itallia, is, in Valdez's own words, "a beached whale," while Jorge Bianchi, who once made a personal phone call to Picasso, is often described, again in Valdez's words, as a "dense piece of shredded wheat in the Gobi Desert."

Valdez, D'Itallia, and Bianchi. They were drastically

different, yet they shared one common trait: they all paid attention to Picasso.

Picasso was not interested in men for any one thing that you could define or pin down. As a painter he celebrated the harmony that he saw in some, but not all, of the men in his life. And even if he couldn't see any harmony in some men, he went ahead and celebrated something else about those men.

For Picasso, a man was never, say, "a guy who needs to drop a few." For Picasso every man he saw was there to be broken down. Broken down into line, form, color. The stuff of art.

Picasso *attacked* the artistic problems inherent in men. He continued to do so his entire life, even though almost everybody asked him, at one time or another, to cut it out.

But cut it out he did not. He was never content, never satisifed, always striving.

He was not like other men. He was Picasso.

Fernande Valdez was, for almost eight years, Picasso's mailman. What did the artist mean to Valdez? Let him tell us in his own words.

"I remember once I was coming up to his house, and I could see him standing out in front. He looked real nervous. He was watching me very carefully while I put his mail in his box. Just staring at me. His house was way up on a hill, but his box was down on the road, so he had a hell of a long walk to get his mail. I could never understand that setup. The man's a famous artist. He's loaded. Yet his mailbox has gotta be like a hundred yards from his house! You figure it out.

"Anyway, as soon as I close the mailbox, here comes Picasso, bustin' tail down the hill to get his mail. Right away I know he's going to be disappointed because all he has in his box is three bills and a *National Geographic.*

"I get over to the next box and I hear these feet *pounding* behind me. I turn around and yeah, it's Picasso. He was an old man when I knew him, but he could really motor. In bare feet, too. I understand why they call him great.

"Right away he asks me if I'm sure I delivered all his mail. Now I'm sure, but I go ahead and look in my bag anyway. I always do that. It makes people feel good.

"After I got finished 'looking' I told him, 'Sorry, Picasso. No dice. Maybe tomorrow.'

"I walked away, but when I got to the next box I caught a glimpse of him over my shoulder. He was standing right where I left him. He was completely still. That image has always stayed with me somehow. The old artist in his shorts, standing like a statue under the Spanish sky. Looking at him I felt in touch with emotions I had never felt so clearly before. Emotions of human suffering, human loss, human disappointment.

"Thinking back on this, I'm pretty sure he must have been looking for a check."

Marcel D'Itallia was Picasso's garbageman for over a decade, a decade in which Picasso produced some of his most memorable works, while D'Itallia almost doubled his salary. D'Itallia reveals another side of the multifaceted enigma that is Picasso.

"He was a wild man! I don't think the guy *had* a shirt!

58

"He was always staring at the truck, like he was study-ing it. Maybe he was going to paint a picture of it. If he was, I never saw the picture. I will tell you it was a hell of a good-looking truck.

"I remember Picasso's face would light up when we yelled 'Power!' and turned on the crusher. He would get on his feet and laugh and laugh, like he was having the time of his life. He'd be waving, whistling, jumping up and down. He was just like a big kid.

"Picasso wasn't an easy man to understand, but there was one thing you could always count on with him. He always had a *lot* of garbage. He had three of these big oversized cans and they were always packed. Like two, three hundred pounds of garbage every week. I must have asked him a *hundred* times to use plastic bags, but he never did. I finally *gave* him some bags. Still, he never used them. Probably threw them away somewhere.

"Some days, Christ, it felt like he'd poured cement into those cans.

"He may have been a great artist, but he was not what you would call a very cooperative customer."

Finally there is Jorge Bianchi, a telephone salesperson who once made a phone call to Picasso. Even though Bianchi is a man, he still refers to himself as a "sales-person." As you might expect from such a person, Bian-chi's version of Picasso is bizarre, eccentric. Yet do not *all* views count when we are talking about somebody like Picasso? Certainly Bianchi has a voice, and it is a voice that deserves to be heard.

"I didn't even notice at first that I was calling Pablo Picasso. They give you this big list of names, and they have it all written out, what they want you to say. I called Picasso on a Tuesday morning, I think. I remember my stomach was growling. That's all I remember, if you're talking about specifics.

"So I'm there with the phone on my shoulder waiting for the jerk on the other end to pick it up. Then it hit me. It hit me while I was thinking about saying, 'Hello, can I speak to Pablo Picasso, please?'

"This was *Pablo Picasso* here. I'm going to be talking to him. Me.

"Anyway, I said the same things I always said, the words from the card they gave us, and Picasso hung up before I even got to the part about the steak knives.

"I think he was overrated."

In the Moors
for the Season

"You've got no mountains in England," said Alan
King, an alumnus of the Catskill comic circuit who
stood up firmly, mock-nasty at times, for America's
reputation for fun. "You can't be funny in the
moors."

—*The New York Times*

There was one impression that was inescapable. Over
Wuthering Heights there was a brooding horror, a great
darkness, a still, almost morbid quality that pervaded
the very air. The place itself was a sort of mirror image
of the manor's master. Even today, the very sound of
the man's name evokes a sense of vast, fog-shrouded
moors and Stygian hidden passageways.

Heathcliff. Intense. Dark-browed. Brooding. One of
the fastest guys with a one-liner anywhere.

In all of England I don't believe I could have found a
place farther removed from society. A misanthropist's
heaven! And Mr. Heathcliff, what an impressive figure

he is! He little suspects how he affects people with his black eyes and his thick scowling brows!

I rode up to him today and greeted him. He responded in that same manner he always adopted, distant, troubled, aloof. I asked him if he even *liked* my company, and he asked me what company I was with.

He had his demons. Deeply buried, brooding demons.

Wuthering Heights was the name of Mr. Heathcliff's dwelling, "wuthering" being a significant provincial adjective, descriptive of the atmospheric tumult to which its station is exposed in stormy weather.

Before passing the threshold of this melancholy edifice, I paused to admire a quantity of grotesque carving over the principal door. I could make out, among a wilderness of crumbling mythological creatures, the date "1500." I dared to ask the surly owner of the place for a short history. He turned suddenly and I saw his dark eyes blaze. I knew I had to change the subject quickly. I groped for words. I had seen the stables on the way in, and I asked him if he had been riding that day. He nodded.

"Horseback?" I ventured timidly.

"Oh, sure," said the melancholy owner of the manor. "We came back together."

Then he walked over to the nearest window and stood staring off into the distant gloom.

We dined that evening in the cavernous moody dining hall. I remember asking Heathcliff if he wanted frogs' legs, and he said he liked his legs the way they were. This was typical of him. Dark-browed, scowling. More like a visitor from the deep caverns of damnation than a polite dinner host.

Today set in, misty and cold. I had half a mind to spend it by my study fire instead of wading through heath and mud to gloomy Wuthering Heights. But I rose and, girding myself against the elements, dutifully walked to the melancholy manor, which the weather made look even more melancholy than usual, if you can believe it.

Heathcliff greeted me at the door, if opening the door and standing there can be construed as a greeting. I was very tired from my journey, and I asked for a room and a bath. Heathcliff said that I could have a room, but I'd have to take my own bath.

Brooding. Dark. What other adjectives are possible to describe this man?

Two events in his early life seemed, to a large extent, to have shaped Heathcliff's character. Catherine, the girl he loved, had been attacked by a dog early in his life, but when I asked him about it he was as grim and stolid about that as he was about everything else. Once, in a quiet moment, I asked him what should be done about biting dogs.

He sat brooding for a full minute before he turned and spoke in a calm voice that did little to mask the seething rage behind it.

"Don't bite any," he said.

Then he returned to his brooding.

The other formative incident in Heathcliff's life involved his being banished from his home and forced to live outside like a wild animal. This treatment only served to make him even darker and more brooding than he would have been normally. When I knew him, he would walk outside in the worst weather and prowl the grounds like a man possessed. Once, while a bitter storm raged, I saw him walking, without so much as a coat, out in front of the manor. Putting on a heavy slicker, I went out after him. His eyes met mine. His black orbs were so fierce, so disdainful of nature itself. His hair and clothes were soaked with the pelting rain, and his sharp, almost canine teeth gleamed in defiance and wrath.

I begged him to come inside to a warm fire. His response was a sort of guttural expression of disregard for all the niceties of "civilized" life.

"It's so late," I shrieked. "It's twenty to three!"

He turned slowly. Our eyes met.

"Really?" he screamed. "Who's winning?"

I left him there, a savage, atavistic creature standing alone in the pitiless, raging storm.

The next night we dined as if nothing had happened. Conversation, as always with Heathcliff, was sparse. We were nearing the end of our meal when he suddenly went into a fit of uncontrollable coughing, no doubt a result of last night's behavior.

I asked him whether he was doing anything for his cough.

"Why should I?" he said, the candlelight playing menacingly over his dark countenance. "It's not doing anything for me."

And another dark, brooding dinner came to an end.

For a man so seemingly secure in life, Heathcliff showed a side of him that was still very much the terror-stricken child he had been. For instance, he insisted, on all occasions, that he be the one to answer the door. He wouldn't let the servants go near the door. Once there was a knock and as always, the master of the house rose to answer it. When he returned, Heathcliff was holding some papers. I asked him if the caller had been a man with a bill.

Heathcliff's eyes blazed and his brow darkened.

"No," he said. "Just a regular nose."

Now, as I look over the melancholy, timeless moors, my mind moves back to thoughts of Heathcliff and his Catherine, up in the cemetery, together forever, a few scant feet from each other. I knew, somehow, what Heathcliff would say.

"Sometimes I wish we were dead."

Southern Living: One Man's Story

I have been living for thirty-four years, and most of it is what you would call Southern living. I've spent a lot of time thinking about how best to decorate with my weed eater. And then, afterward, I spent a long time trying to think of a "clever title" for what I did with the weed eater.

After a while, it got to be an obsession, this "clever title" thing. At night these things would float into my brain and disturb me, even if I took the precaution of heavily sedating myself.

SAGE ADVICE ABOUT HERBS

THE POSSUM: FEW DIE OF
OLD AGE

MY HOT DATES WITH A
CHICKEN IN THE COUNTRY

I DON'T LIKE MARGARET
THATCHER, BUTTER BEANS
ARE FINE

After several years of Southern living I found myself doing little else except feeding the maid chess pie and making sure to mulch everything I saw. I thought of little else except where to hide my family while they came over and took pictures of my house.

I look back at those years now, and I try to forget. I try to forget but I can't. There is always that picture. It's always out there. Lurking, waiting to turn up. The possibility of that picture turning up has kept me completely out of politics and partially out of many other things.

That picture. Me. In an Izod and khakis. *Me.*

In front of a rich background of magnolias.

That's what it says: "Here he is in front of a rich background of magnolias."

I'm not proud, but I'm not ashamed to tell the truth. At one time in my life my porch was very important to me. I would stare at my porch and think, Yeah.

My whole sense of self-worth was tied into my lawn. Today I can look at my old phone book and see the shocking truth: under "numbers frequently called" I have the numbers for Leisure Lawn, Barefoot Grass, Chemlawn, and Green City.

I can remember long sleepless nights alone in my bed, fighting the almost uncontrollable urge to go outside and pet my azaleas.

I can joke about it now, but fescue was more important to me than sex with my spouse, at one time.

At one time I preferred the company of hardy eupatorium to the company of my family and loved ones.

There seemed to be no end to my illness. I remember telling my wife that I was going into my office to work on the income tax. Then I remember shutting the door, locking it, and then taking out my "private stock," lurid photographs of squills, daffodils, and other small spring-flowering bulbs.

There was one weekend in particular that even now I can't recall without trembling. I drove to a distant city, checked in to a motel under an assumed name, and spent thirty-six consecutive hours looking at open floor plans and master suites! There was plenty of stucco, too. And, near the end of my little binge, I looked at twenty consecutive pages of fireplace and bath additions!

Who was this person who did all this? Today I can look at me in those days as if I were some stranger, some alien, perhaps. But I must never pretend that it wasn't me because it was.

I'm past the denial stage and I know that there is hope for me and hope for so many others who have been through this same hell. Today I can truly say that I am able to lead a normal healthy life, except during the leaf season.

The
Defense
Rests

It is not my habit to employ duplicity or artifice. But
I want to make it clear that I am not Billy Budd.
                              —New York Mayor Ed Koch

I always see him the same way in my mind's eye. Arms
upraised, striped tie, astride the yardarm end, foot in
stirrup, confronting the wackos. Very much the picture
of the young Alexander, but feistier, and his hairline is
different.

One would think him to be the perfect image of the
romantic sailor of song and tale.

Alas, his tale is no romance.

What could I know of this man except as a sailor? This
Claggart, or whatever his name was. Captain Vere is a
sailor too, and he's an honorable man. Not overly in-
telligent, but honorable.

They call me the "handsome sailor."

What do I think about that?

I won't be influenced by flattery. I tell them they should save it for their mothers.

Now what is all this that these people are saying about me?

"Mustering the men for mutiny." These people expect me to take them seriously? What do I look like, the serial killer?

Look, I'm not perfect. I stutter. I stammer. Sure. I'm a human being.

I hit this idiot Claggart in the forehead. Sure. I always like to tweak people. With me, what you see is what you get.

Let me say this.

God bless Captain Vere.

Maybe what happened was unfortunate. Maybe it should have never happened at all. But Claggart? The man was *meshugge*. He got just what he deserved.

Maybe we need more police on navy boats. Maybe we wouldn't have this situation if we did. But let me ask you this. Do you want to pay more taxes?

Maybe not.

All right, so I don't talk well. I stammer and stutter when I get excited. But this is America. We have all kinds of people here. Lispers. Drawlers. Hemmers. Hawers.

You know what it would be like if everybody spoke properly?

It would be *boring*.

So sure, I hit this total idiot and everybody makes a big *tsimmes* out of it.

Let me sum it up for you . . .

Think of it . . .

Let me say . . .

You'll be interested in knowing . . .

But you'll have to understand . . .

Are you following me . . .

I'm stammering here. That's my problem. We all have problems. We're all individuals, and we all hang on to whatever it is that makes us different from other people who might as well live in the suburbs. People like me stammer. That's part of what makes us what we are. I'm proud that I stammer.

Where are the reporters?

You'll be interested in knowing that I won't be intimidated by a bunch of vile, unforgivable accusations.

Let me sum it up for you.

Claggart and I did not get along. I consider it a compliment that people like him don't like me.

I am not peeved. I am not annoyed. I am just asking to be treated like every other sailor who pays his taxes and keeps his nose clean.

It's clear to me that you aren't familiar with my résumé. I could be a hair shirt and take this lying down, but I won't.

Can you tell me one other sailor in the whole navy who is willing to spill his guts this way?

I don't think so.

As far as this whole thing goes, let me ask you, are all of these people just looking for a cheap headline?

I've been a sailor a long time. But I've lived on the land too. And you know what it's like living on the land? It's nothing. It's sterile. It's like living on a Monopoly board.

It's *boring*.

Hey, if I wanted to placate this Claggart, I could have, but that's not my style. The coin of the realm in the navy is, Get out of way, Heave ho, mateys, all of that *nonsense.* I could walk around saying "avast" and "poop deck." But I don't. That's not my style.

This whole scene isn't as sexy as showing some mob scene on the six o'clock news. I realize that. I realize that more than anybody.

I see Captain Vere over there. Let me tell you something about him. Every time I see Captain Vere I think this button goes off in his brain and he thinks, What would the "handsome sailor" want to hear? That's the way his mind works.

I enjoy being a sailor. Every day is a new adventure. I think that, if nothing else, this hearing shows one thing: I am not going to take any crap from Captain Vere, the navy, or about a hundred and fifty other "important" people I could name.

You have to understand that any time somebody asks me not to do something, I usually go right ahead and do it. Nobody, no matter how "important" he is, tells me what to do.

When I walked in here today I got the feeling that everybody here was hostile to me. It seemed like you would just as soon take me out and hang me from the yardarm, or whatever it is that you fellows call those things. You know what I think about that?

I find it charming.

What
the Russians
Did to My Book

Last year the Soviets got ahold of my book and made it into a made-for-TV movie. Was I happy about this? *Am* I happy about this? The answers are surprising, and they tell us a great deal about the Soviets.

First, in order to understand what the Soviets did to my book, you should know the basic plot of the book the way I wrote it.

Edward Tang, a small-town classics professor, is swept into a world of international turmoil when he begins dating the beautiful and alluring Jenny Dystad. On their first date he takes her to a movie, and afterward they go out for a couple of beers. On their second date they go out and see Rich Little. It is after the Little show (the ten o'clock show) that Tang discovers the dark secret that clouds their budding relationship: Jenny Dystad, beautiful and alluring, is also a vampire.

Pamela Berkely, beautiful but tough, is a young, ambitious newspaper woman who personifies the "new woman." Everything about her says NOW. She is the one who stumbles across the real story. The real story is, Bernard Flagler, millionaire philanthropist, is heavily involved in an international baby-selling ring. In this sordid operation, which I describe quite well, the *modus operandi* involves implanting genetic "seeds" in unsuspecting women who think that they're just having their hair done. Nine months later, working through a computer network, Flagler and his cohorts reap their ghastly harvest. No one is the wiser and life goes on.

Flagler is married to Marjorie "Bonnie" Burger, heiress to a vast rubber-gloves fortune. She has so much money she doesn't know what the hell to do with it. She must have the best of everything: the best clothes, the best food, the best cars, the best dentist. She just doesn't know any other way to live.

Unbeknownst to his wife, Flagler has, for a number of years, been carrying on a torrid affair with Meredith Reamer, beautiful and mysterious but with shady underworld connections. Meredith Reamer sometimes doesn't need to have the best of everything. Sometimes, just for the heck of it, she'll go to a drive-through place for lunch and eat in her car, but she doesn't make a habit of it.

Finally the police arrive and stage a bloody shootout. This is near the end.

Flagler, his empire crumbling around him, leaps from a window at his palatial estate. He lands, shoulder-rolls to the ground, and comes up firing. The SWAT team opens up and there's a hail of flesh-rending bullets everywhere. They get Flagler. He's dead. Everybody else is okay.

THE END

My novel was translated into thirty-seven languages, including Urdu, Coptic, and Goanese. It sold over seventy-one million copies worldwide. Among the Natuna islanders, it created a sensation. In the Bordeaux region of France, people were lined up around the block waiting for a chance to buy a copy.

I was pleased. My book was a success. But I was not prepared for the phone call I got on Thursday afternoon, August 16, 1984. The Soviet Union was going to make my book into a made-for-TV movie!

Although I had second thoughts, curiosity got to me, and I went ahead and made the deal. I wondered, What *would* Communist Russia do to my book?

I soon found out.

I went to a lot of trouble talking on the phone with the Russians, but I was finally able to get a videotape of the TV movie. The tape was in Russian, of course, but I watched it with a friend of mine who speaks Russian. We sat together and watched the whole thing, and he translated. I had mentally prepared myself for changes because I know the way that Russians always are about everything, but I was *not* prepared for what I saw.

Whatever was on that screen, it certainly wasn't my book!

First of all, the Soviets made Pamela Berkely have

black hair! I couldn't believe what I was seeing. Here's how I describe her in the book:

"Her bronzed skin glistened and her mane of gleaming *blond hair* [italics added] gently swayed in the tropical breeze."

Yet here I was, sitting and watching Pamela Berkely, and she's got just jet-black hair. Not even brown. Unbelievable.

That was just the beginning. Bernard Flagler, whom I described as "doesn't wear glasses," was wearing glasses through the whole movie. Not rimless jobs, either. Big tortoise-shell ones! I had written, "Edward Tang really had a bushy mustache. His friends used to kid him about it," but I guess our Communist "friends" forgot that little detail too. The actor playing Tang looked like he just finished shaving. He didn't even have a little stubble!

I could go on, but you get the idea. By the time I had finished watching the movie, I was almost overcome by a gnawing feeling of emptiness.

I did gain something from the whole ordeal: a new respect for the American system. Things like what happened to my book just don't happen in a free country. I've stopped taking America for granted.

The Price
You Gotta Pay

America's future rests in a thousand dreams inside
your hearts. It rests in the message of hope in songs
of a man so many young Americans admire—New
Jersey's own Bruce Springsteen. And helping you
make those dreams come true is what this job of mine
is all about.

> —President Reagan, quoted in *People*

From the Commissioner

There have been a number of changes on this year's
1040 Federal Income Tax Form and the shorter Form
1040EZ, because of recent legislation and certain re-
quests made by the President. As you no doubt know,
this Administration is committed to making the dreams
of so many young Americans come true.

Nevertheless, be sure to report all of your earnings
and income. In all fairness to the vast majority of tax-
payers who voluntarily comply with the tax laws, we
must continue to seek out those of you who lie to us.
Please don't lie to us; we're sure you won't. Look, everybody's got a secret, but you can't carry it with you every

step you take. Someday you're gonna have to cut it loose or let it drag you down.

Understating your income will be more costly for you because of interest penalties in addition to the afore-mentioned burden of carrying said secret.

Thank you for your cooperation.

In This Year's Form

1. If you have been and are still working all day in your daddy's garage, and you have gotten up every morning and gone to work each day, you may qualify for an additional personal exemption. Note: If your eyes have gone blind and your blood runs cold, see instructions for "Medical and Dental Payments" on page 19.

2. A person who sells (or otherwise transfers) an interest in a tax shelter must attach Form 4133 in completed form to this return. Note: You may omit Form 4133 if you talk only to strangers and walk with angels that have no place and you don't care anymore. (See instructions, page 23.)

3. Investment losses are treated differently this year. For more information and details obtain Publication 463, "Out on Highway 9, Where Dreams Are Found and Lost," available at your post office, or order from your regional tax office.

4. Some of the deductions for medicine and drugs have been changed. If you can't use all of the medical expenses on Form 2441 because of the earned-income limitation and you're running on the bad side and got your back to the wall, you

may still be entitled to take additional allowances for expenses incurred in renovating your personal vehicle if it meets the following criteria:

a. Your non-business vehicle has a 396 (350 permissible for California) with fuelie heads.

b. You and your partner Sonny built said vehicle straight out of scratch.

c. You have met the qualification with said vehicle by takin' all the action you can meet. (See Schedule 11: "Shutdown Strangers Rumbling Through This Promised Land.")

d. You have, throughout the tax year, ridden roads till dawn, wasted on something in the night. (Attach Schedule 344: "Forgotten or Forgiven Credits.")

5. If you spent at least six months of the tax year workin' in the fields until you got your back burned, you may be eligible for special agricultural-induced disability tax credits. (See Schedule 177: "Badlands and Freeze-Outs.")

Personal Deduction Changes

• You may take an additional deduction for your baby if she's got wrinkles 'round her eyes now and she cries herself to sleep at night. Note: You may claim this deduction only if *both* criteria—babyhood and wrinkles—are met. Also, said situation must meet the tests described elsewhere on this page under "Married Persons who Live Apart" (i.e., *Things You Just Can't Live Down*), and you must provide documentation to that effect.

- If during the tax year you and your spouse were full-time students at an institution of higher education in the United States, you may claim a tax credit if either spouse was, while an enrolled student, simultaneously payin' for the sins of somebody else's past. You may not, however, use any sums paid as tuition to a college or technical school to figure in any tax credit unless you can provide documentation to prove that you also spent at least six consecutive weeks of the tax year walkin' empty rooms lookin' for something to blame. (See instructions, page 32: "Head of Household Empty Room Rollovers.")

- Credit may be taken for certain fuels from a nonconventional source. (See instructions, page 14: "Hemi-Powered Drones and Last-Chance Power Drive Option.")

Miscellaneous Expenses You Cannot Deduct

☐ Political contributions. (But see instructions for Form 1040, line 44.)

☐ Your daddy's Cadillac.

☐ Certain "freeze-out" legal fees.

☐ Metallic depreciation. (See instructions, page 13: "Rat Traps, Lined Circuits, and Chromed Invaders.")

☐ Local and state gasoline taxes paid while driving sleek machines over the Jersey state line.

☐ Expenses incurred while blowing away the dreams

that break your heart (unless documentation is provided of complete breakage).

☐ Expenses incurred while acquiring income eligible for partial taxation via Tier 1 Railroad Retirement Benefits. (See instructions, page 10: "Screams into the Night.")

John Stern: American Man

The man is John Stern. John Stern. An American man. He was born in America. If it can be arranged, he's going to die in America. His wife is an American girl who is even more American than John Stern because she's from the real heartland of America.

She's a feminine woman and she might fool you with her looks, but if you took a few hours to mull it over you would see that looks can fool you. She's about as weak as a car-crushing, fuel-burning funnycar.

John Stern and his woman. They're standing tall and they're not alone. They have these kids. Three of them. A boy and two girls. American kids. Kids who grow. Grow to walk, talk, and think like Americans. They hang around with other American kids and they know that the future of America comes from playgrounds like theirs. It goes around and slides down. It gets dirt all over itself. The future stands in line for a water break.

John Stern used to drive a foreign car. Before he noticed that the pride was back and he didn't have to do anything stupid anymore. Now he drives American.

Because that's what he is. He can feel the feeling. It's a good feeling. Now that the pride is back.

He likes to drink beer. A hell of a lot of beer. A hell of a lot of American beer. Just a really great amount of beer, as long as most of it, anyway, is American. Just a *ton* of beer. He's got that feeling that says, "I feel good." He feels good about beer. And good about America and its role in beer. He likes to go to a place where you can buy a person a beer and look in his eye, and brother, you made a friend. And that person he made a friend of will come over to his house and take care of the children while he and his woman go out.

And, when he and his woman come back, after drinking a lot of beer, John Stern knows that he can look his friend right in the eye, shake his hand, and his friend will go home. Around here, you don't say much but what you say you mean.

But there's just one more thing. John Stern is mad. Fighting mad. How mad? Mad enough.

They did John Stern wrong. They gave him a bum steer. They talked out of both sides of their mouth. They played him for a sucker. They told him to roll over and play dead. They said, "Stick out your hand and shake, John Stern. Good boy." They pulled the rug out from underneath John Stern. They flim-flammed him. They shook him down.

They did him wrong.

Now John Stern is coming back. And he's coming back *mad*.

His wife left him because she was stuck in a job that didn't allow her to grow. She was polo. He was racetrack.

JOHN STERN: AMERICAN MAN

He was wall-to-wall carpeting. She was the hardwood floor they discovered underneath.

She ran him through a real miniature golf course. Up the ramp to the dinosaur mouth. Past the swinging lobster claw. Between the spastic mice. Down the big yellow funnel to the clown's blinking nose.

It was the whole gamut. But he wasn't the first.

She was the gentle side of him. Now she's gone.

John Stern is still here.

Who is John Stern? He's just a regular guy. He puts in a forty-hour week. He doesn't think he's anything special. He keeps asking for raises and he stays out sick a lot.

He's just another Joe. But, you know what? He's proud of what he is. And you ask him that and he'll tell you that. Mister.

He's not a hothead. He doesn't fly off the handle. But when something like what happened happens to him, it looks like a whole new ball game. It looks like John Stern. John Stern alone. John Stern alone on a mindless rampage.

John Stern alone on a mindless rampage of revenge and death.

John Stern. This time he's not taking no for an answer. This time he's not taking "Thank you for your application. Many times because of various factors, we have to turn down business that we would normally want to have. Yours is just such a case. We thank you very much and wish you good luck elsewhere."

John Stern is tired of taking it. Now he's giving it back.

This time everybody is going to be sorry.

William "The Refrigerator" Perry is going to cry his head off.

Chuck Norris plans to wail his lamentations into the still, black night.

The "Big Chill" generation isn't going to be completely happy about it.

Malcolm Forbes is going to send a note.

But this time sorry isn't good enough.

John Stern has trained hard. He knows what it's like when your veins pop out and your blood screams and your hamstrings drag you into court and sue you for every cent you're worth. He knows what it's like to spend his vacation in a cement mixer of agony. He's been around the track. He's street-smart. He knows the ropes.

John Stern. He was in Europe last summer, but now he's back. Back where he belongs. Back in America.

He's doing what he has to do, and what he has to do is pay the bills. Call him a jerk. Call him a dinosaur. Say he doesn't belong. Say he's a throwback. Say he's got his head in the sand. Say his time has passed.

He'll give you a one-word answer. Mister. And you can take that answer to the bank. Don't expect a free toaster when you get there, though. The time for free toasters is over. Mister.

Pretext
for
a Gathering

Fortunately, the panel discussions at the PEN congress, like the panel discussions at a convention of aluminum siding salesmen, are merely a pretext for a gathering of people engaged in the same business in different places.   —*People,* February 3, 1986

He is as tall as a side of lap siding turned sideways. His demeanor is still as watertight as ever, even after so many years. His walk may have slowed, his chin's become a little weak, but when he opens his mouth to speak, he's watertight. As if his whole body had, at one time or another, been dipped in caulking compound.

He is Charles "Bevels" Nutly, seventy-seven, the grand old man of siding. He walks to the dais in the lush MEETING room of the Clarkesville Holiday Inn. No matter where you're sitting you can feel the respect that his simple presence evokes. He had been a legend in siding and he was still here. In his long career he had worn all the Yeatsian masks: contractor, manufacturer, distributor, repairer, installer. It was a career that would have turned a lesser man into a sheet-rocker long ago. Yet here he was, still here, addressing maybe fifty-two people—aluminum siding people, the real practitioners, and the rest: enthusiasts, dilettantes, students, hangers-on, thrill seekers.

"In the next few days," he says in same familiar, raspy voice, "let's not forget that alumnium siding, above all else, is supposed to be fun. Let's not turn this thing into a mass for the dead. Have fun! Get loaded!"

Nutly's optimistic message was not heeded for long. The aluminum-siding mini-convention swiftly turned into a grotesque circus of innuendo, aspersions, chicanery, booby traps, and mummery.

Sam Saye, the titular chairman, was the next to speak after Nutly. Saye got things rolling by inviting, as a guest speaker, his brother-in-law, Herb Finan, a well-known downspout-lengthening specialist. Many of Saye's colleagues, making no secret of their hostility toward drainage systems, greeted Finan's speech with catcalls and heckling. The crowd got worse and worse. Saye finally had to publicly apologize for the crowd to Finan, and Finan, always the good sport, went back to his room, packed, and left.

After "the Finan thing," as one hanger-on called it, there was a brief respite.

This respite, regrettably, was short-lived.

Soon, two rival factions made themselves known. The larger and probably the more powerful was the "make your home a model showcase home for a reduced price" group. Headed by vinyl king Murray Bellah, they seemed to be everywhere. Their dominance was not by any means guaranteed, however. There was the eccentric Mort

"Durowall" Wainscott and his group, the "siding for interior use can be an offbeat architectural asset" sect. They dressed upscale, but they weren't above hurling invectives. They weren't above hurling prefabricated trusses, if it came to that, and it almost did, several times.

There were those who sought a judicious truce, among them John "Scratchcoat" Lippett. "We are here in the name of siding. And siding alone. We are not trying to solve the problems of the world."

For his judiciousness, Lippett was rewarded with a drip cap hurled by an irate factionist.

"You're a real prince," said Lippett, who hurried off the dais, packed, and left.

Although insurgency was the order of the day, it was hard to top Ohio's own John Graham. Attired in a wild, attention-getting manner that one bystander described as "anti-drip compound," Graham took his place on the dais and pronounced, "Let's face it. Nobody in this room cares about anything but sending out little mailers and pestering somebody until he finally goes ahead, and then coming out to his house very early and waking him up. Then after he's awake, you put up five or six strips of siding and leave. Then you never show up for a week and you get a stupid person to answer your phone."

Graham's excessive polemics were, alas, typical of the extremist faction in the room. Some observers wondered why many of the more vocal participants among the extreme faction hadn't just gotten into something else, like roofing clips. Something more practical.

Some foreign aluminium-siding people decried what they considered the growing trend toward tunnel vision in American siding practices. As one foreigner put it,

"Maybe it is something in the nature of your country, but when I look at the aluminum siding that is being installed in America, I can't help but think, 'Sure, it's good, but what does it tell me?' Very competent, very well installed. Very professional. But it only speaks to my mind."

There were voices of sanity. In a memorable moment, forty-nine-year-old Henry Pfiester, tottering now, but with a brave voice, told those assembled, "Siding used to be a pure profession. We took siding and sheathing and we undersunk the nails and that was that."

Suddenly the room grew silent.

"We've lost our roots," he said.

There was not a sound in the room as Pfiester left the dais and went to the men's room.

Despite all this, the mini-convention did not turn into a mass for the dead. Drinks. They were everywhere. Tanks and tonics and more tanks and tonics. Good talk. Talk of window swellings and furring strips. Of extractor screws and copper flashing. Good hard talk. Fueled by alcohol and relieved from the burden of "official" postures, aluminum-siding salesmen showed themselves to be just that: people who sold aluminum siding. Underline people.

As time went on, the people at the mini-convention began to see similarities rather than differences in their colleagues. One estimable siding cynosure said, "People who work with siding are a different breed. When we put up, say, a Dutch Colonial effect, and there aren't any dents in it, and you know that it's going to outlast the structural members of the house . . . well, it makes you a little nuts. Getting together like this with these other aluminum-siding people, it really helps you get rid of the demons."

For all of the screaming and ranting, when the mini-convention ended, many expressed a note of regret that the whole thing was over. "I loved the discussions," said Larry Karp, a siding contractor from Ohio and one of the hot new stars on the aluminum-siding horizon. "Do you own your own home?"

Then it was all over and everybody left. They all left the artificial world of the mini-convention and went back to what was, after all, the very fiber of their lives: giant stacks of little mailers, plenty of nails and set screws, and, more than anything else, that thing we call aluminum siding.

Kudzu East
and West
and South

This is how it starts.

DOWN HERE WE HAVE THIS PLANT. A VINE, ACTU-ALLY. IT HAS A KIND OF EXOTIC, FOREIGN-SOUNDING NAME TO IT.

This is, of course, by now enough to make you sick. You've picked up the paper and started reading another goddamn story about kudzu.

Such a whimsical subject, kudzu.

There have been, at this point, a great number of articles and columns about kudzu. In Southern news-papers, for instance, an informal survey placed the num-ber of kudzu articles at "no lower than 32,000 and no higher than a googolplex."

These are all humorous columns, and we love seeing them in the paper. But they all say the same thing: kudzu grows very fast and it is hard to get rid of. That's the deal with kudzu. What else can you say?

But what is the attitude in the ancestral home of

kudzu? Does the Eastern world approach the subject of this vine in the same manner?

The answer turns out to be no.

I live in Tallulah Falls, Georgia. We have kudzu here, but my attitude toward it is far different from the Japanese attitude. Let me show you what I mean. Here's a Japanese guy writing about kudzu.

> The rice plant bows
> But not the kudzu
> Get out and burn it, Yukio

Has any poem ever offered a clearer expression of the contrast between East and West?

Consider this haiku. It was written in the seventeenth century, but it speaks like today's headlines.

> Rain sings softly
> That's no excuse
> Get out there, Yukio

Yet one does not have to renounce all earthly goods and move to India and kneel motionless on the soft grass for three years in order to appreciate kudzu. Whatever else it is, and it's probably plenty, the vine is not something that can be easily dealt with, especially by a contemplative type.

> Wonder and ecstasy
> Birds make music
> Get busy, Yukio

Kudzu is many things to many people: a dance, a gladdening of the heart, a summons, a subpoena.

There have been many haikus written on kudzu. They can be appreciated individually, but perhaps their fullest sense can be absorbed when they are read en masse.

Consider this brilliant series, written long ago but on the same afternoon.

I

What this is
I do not know
There is a hell of a lot of it

II

A green vine
With dense leaves
Young man, stop resting

III

A frog looks
The leaves breathe
Get your blowtorch

IV

Shaven-headed Buddhist monks
Appreciate the good work
You are doing with that blowtorch

V

The moon is a kudzu vine
Frozen
In blue ice

VI
The memory of the mirror
Is covered in kudzu vines
It's time to get busy again

A man is like a kudzu vine. He starts out as narrow, self-centered, isolated. His world is a small one. He is an angry little guy. Soon, though, he grows and grows. He covers everything. He becomes boundless. His reach seems infinite. He has his little grubby fingers in everything.

We react. We take the man and have him indicted. We chop the vine down and throw it in the fire. Then we send the man to prison, so that he also "knows his place."

This is the way of kudzu.

Aspects
of the
TV Show

First may I say how grateful I am to be asked to give these lectures. A look at the past names associated with this lectureship both flatters and humbles me.

That being said, my subject is a subject that greater minds than mine have approached before. My subject is "The TV Show."

Before beginning, we need a vantage point, for the field of TV shows is so vast and formidable. It is a vast swamp of hours and half hours and even some quarter hours, if you get up early enough. It is a thick, semi-liquid morass of sitcoms, cops, bathing suits, and concerned doctors. I am not surprised at the mental exhaustion of TV critics. Imagine attempting to evaluate, for once and for all, *The Baileys of Balboa* and *S.W.A.T.* Or staring with a critical, cold eye at the six beautiful lady truckers. Or an evening spent in exegesis following the interrogation of the newlyweds.

How can any critical mind, no matter how subtle, be equal to the task?

But try I will.

Looking over this vast expanse that is our subject, we can see that some parts are clearer than others. The mind can conceive of this: there is a desk with a man behind it. To his right there are chairs. The chairs are filled with actors. They sit and talk. Then someone goes over to the band and does a song. He returns. Another man comes out and talks standing up for about four minutes. He sits down. A man comes out who has written a book. He too sits down. He starts to talk. We turn it off and go to bed.

What do we make of all this? The critical sensibility begins to work. What was this? An allegory? An exemplum? A Noh play? No. It is, we say, a Talk Show.

Thus, by fits and starts, we stumble on our critical path.

There are a variety of approaches a critic may take. He may look at it chronologically—from *Gilligan's Island* to *The Dukes of Hazzard,* for an example—and comment on the collateral facts, swinging wide and far over the commercials, the time slots, the big yuks, etc. He may talk about genre: shows about cars, shows about bears, shows about people. But what does all this say to us, really? Can the rapture we feel in watching a really good *B.J. and the Bear* really be captured in a critical discourse?

I think not. Ah, I know not.

One thing we can do is to consider one particular

show as a sort of Parnassus from which we may look down on the surrounding shows. The show I have in mind is a show I have long felt an attachment to and an inclination toward. As you know, my close friends and I have for some time felt that our lives were becoming indistinguishable from the lives of the characters on the TV show *Dallas*.

Southfork. It is there we place our Parnassus.

Dallas is, we see, after years of faithful viewing, as multifarious as life itself. It can be wistful, as when Miss Ellie walks in the garden musing about the peaceful effect that flowers have on her (and she can really use that, if you haven't watched the show). It can be moving, as when someone wonders about "puttin' down roots or jes' movin' on."

There are perhaps two major keys: personal and impersonal. But you must also have genius or neither tone will profit. On *Dallas* we have genius in both keys.

PERSONAL: "Where did she go? I'll tell you where. Anywhere in Dallas where she can get a drink."

IMPERSONAL: "Wee hah!"

PERSONAL: "Where is she? I'll tell you where she is. In bed. Drunk."

IMPERSONAL: "Ride 'em!"

PERSONAL: "I knew your daddy and he was lower than a rattlesnake feigning humility." (I am paraphrasing here. The exact metaphor used on the show escapes me, but what I have written conveys the sense of the original if not, alas, its precise verbiage.)

Despite my shortcomings, the point is clear. Has any show so delineated the range of the modern consciousness?

A word here about history. One must tip one's hat to the passing parade, but one must not necessarily pick up a baton and join the ranks. A show, even a show of genius, exists in a certain epoch. Yet it is pseudo-scholarship at its worst if we relate everything on *Dallas* to the parade passing behind it. All works of genius belong to a common state that it is convenient to call "inspiration." With regard to that state, we may say, "History develops; Art stands still." The question of whether or not Sue Ellen will win custody of her son even though she has just been released from a sanitarium where she endured mind-bending withdrawal from booze—this is a timeless question. The question of whether J.R. will become fatally captivated by a beautiful but evil oil executive working for a ruthless Greek magnate with sunglasses—this is a question for the ages.

These aspects of the show are quite aloof from the ephemera that we call today's headlines. When we have completely forgotten Ronald Reagan, or whatever his name is, the oil baron's ball will continue to burn with a gemlike flame. Especially that look that Jenna gave Pam. We know that's not going anywhere.

One more thing. The human heart. *Dallas,* like all great art, is literally sogged with humanity and there is no avoiding it. We may hate humanity, but if we exorcise it from our critical approach we are left with almost nothing: nothing but row after row of little dots.

I submit to you that a TV show is more than that. It is a man telling his wife that their son is "a little pistol." It is a man startling a woman with his cold hands at a cocktail party and then telling her, "Cold hands, warm heart!" It is a man turning to another man and telling him, "I think it's high time we stopped pretending that everything's all right in this family, because it's not."

I'd like to go on, but it's almost nine and we're all going over to Clive Bell's to watch. He's made dip.

The Nevada Gaming Commission Great Books Program

States are paying some of the best minds in the gambling industry to devise new ways of enticing their citizens to bet more money more often.

—*Harper's,* July 1983

Onstage, the band is ready. The house lights are dimmed. No drinks will be served from this point on. No one will be admitted and no one will leave. The air is heavy with expectancy.

You take a look around the crowd. No tuxes. No bangles. No beads. Lots of herringbone and corduroy. Some argyle. A whole gang of horn rims and a big herd of Hush Puppies.

Nevada, like every other gambling mecca, had realized that it was neglecting one important group: intellectuals. Eggheads and their dollars were once no-line; now they would be forgotten no longer. No, not forgotten, not by a long shot. Under the new approach, they would be enticed and seduced. This evening was theirs, and it was cooking.

Now, all is still. As still as a crowd of sophomores before they get hit with a big metaphysics written.

Somebody coughs.

Then a spotlight comes on and the band comes to life. They growl out a few chords.

Just as suddenly as anything, moving swiftly and economically, he strides onstage. Under the bright lights, he looks like everything we had hoped for. He is about five-foot-eight, but he appears shorter because he is horribly overweight and has bad posture. His hair is a wiry gray, and he doesn't even seem to bother combing it. His suit is a brown unpressed one that he bought off the rack in the early sixties. His tie has a coffee stain on it, right near the knot.

He is everything we hoped for.

While the big band vamps behind him, he looks out at the audience. You think, Is it the air conditioning or did it just get chilly in here? Is he going to put his hands up, stop the band, and ask somebody one of his well-known embarrassing "Platonic method" questions?

No. This is Vegas, not Harvard. He's not into the heavies tonight. Tonight it says "groove" on the sign outside. And that's just what he does. He opens his mouth, but what comes out isn't that Old Man Eloquent:

THE NEVADA GAMING COMMISSION

Come fly with me,
let's fly, let's fly away.
If you can use
some exotic booze,
there's a bar in old Bombay.

He glides effortlessly from standard to standard: "Change Partners," "New Kind of Love," "It Had to Be You." He runs through the whole oeuvre, and one thing becomes very clear in this smoke-filled room:

THE MAN JUST CAN'T SING AT ALL.

He has a range of about a quarter-octave, and every word he "sings" comes right through his nose. Sometimes it makes a sort of whistling noise.

But, you think, *so what?* Why should he know how to sing? The man has never sung, except in church or when drunk, in his entire life. He's really not even an entertainer. In reality, he's a lifelong literary scholar who has written widely on Tennyson, Conrad, and Flaubert. Until four weeks ago he taught comparative literature at a very good university. Now here he is, microphone in hand, belting out:

My story is much too sad to be told.
But nearly everything leaves me totally cold.

Why *did* he leave academia? He certainly wanted a new home. That much is certain. When casinos began to court him, he was not unreceptive to their efforts. Finally, after weeks of negotiations, he accepted. It was good-bye New Haven, hello Las Vegas.

.　　.　　.

I asked Nick Dour, a long-time observer of both casinos and universities, why a noted scholar would make such a career move. He was very willing to talk. He was *too willing* to talk, actually.

"I can understand why he made the move. Here he has everything. Somebody like you, from out of town, you could never understand. But to people here, here we understand things. And notice things."

Much later he told me it was the only place where you could get up, come down for breakfast, and run into Kenny Rogers.

He went on like this for some time.

He finishes his first set with "Quiet Nights, Quiet Stars." Actually, he just gets near the end and starts coughing, but we can all pretty much tell that he's finished.

"Great Jupiter!" he says, after a while, when he can't stop coughing.

Great Jupiter. Over the years it's become his signature line. Even the dead-of-nightskers put their hands together on that one.

He lights up a deathstick and takes a deep drag. He produces a serious drink. He loosens that grayish tie. It's a get-serious time.

"Ladies and gentlemen," he says, raising his glass. "Salut."

With that, just as suddenly as he appeared, he is gone.

And it is time for the Great Books Program. Now, though, he's back.

"You'll notice the screens are the same place they were for the Holmes-Spinks, I've been asked to say."

He stands in that frozen strand of white. We hear one voice. *That* voice.

> 'Scuse me
> While I dis-a-pear

Then he's gone.

THE RED AND THE BLACK

We've got your standard American layout here, thirty-six numbers, each separated by quarter-inch of stainless steel. We've got a single ball-bearing wheel with a four-inch hole in the middle, and the whole deal is balanced on a steel spindle in the middle of a big wooden bowl.

Thirty-six numbers, right? And we pay off at even on a color and thirty-five to one on the numbers.

But check this out. We also have zero and double zero, the two greenies.

Those two greenies feed our children. Without those two little numbers, our hold on life, already fragile, would become nothing less than perilous.

Half of the people would win. Half would lose. The casino, too, would break even. And our children would be driven out into the uncaring Parisian streets, their pathetic cries piercing the very stillness, but falling unheeded and unheard, falling on the eternal black silence of the night.

Zero, double zero. The greenies. We're glad we got 'em.

DAVID COPPERFIELD

Chapter One. I Am Born

Whether I turn out to be the hero of these pages, or it turns out to be that dork Doug Henning, is not for me to say. All I can do is the best possible theatrical magic act.

As for my birth, all I can tell you is that I was born at twelve o'clock on a Friday night, and when my mother turned her head to check out the clock face, what did she see?

That's right. There, impaled on the hour hand, she saw the exact card that she had selected before she had even become pregnant.

And on that card, as a closer look revealed, was written the exact words she had said to my father-to-be when he and my mom first met.

I was a posthumous child. My father died six months earlier. My mother and I were alone in the world. Then the nurse came and said to my mother, "Check the closet."

She did, and there, crouching behind a hound's-tooth overcoat, was my dad. He was safe and sound.

I've never told my mother just how I did it. We never tell. It's part of the code.

I'm on the road a lot now. Vegas. Tahoe. A.C. Yet I still look back fondly to my birth, and how I "pulled this one off."

TOM JONES

Containing much of the birth of a top Las Vegas attraction and still a very popular guy with the ladies.

Chapter One

The author doesn't seek to present himself as the head-liner. He is merely in the lounge. Yet he doesn't expect people to yell obscene stuff at him because they paid a lot of money to get in here and they just had a pretty good dinner and some good hooch.

Tom will be out here any second. The man is a legend. I just saw him backstage. Is he exciting or what?

The man is a legend.

Am I right?

Chapter Two

Now we know each other and I can be a little bit more frank here. It is well known, is it not, that about half of the people in the human race are men in love, am I right? And half are women in love. We're all lovers.

Everybody except you. Tell me, people, do you want to listen to that?

Thank you. And as for you, good luck on your literacy test.

I didn't know Mensa was bringing a bus.

Chapter Three

As I've said earlier, it's a real pleasure to be here and stand in front of you tonight. I did the same thing for my wife last night and she said, "Get out of the way of the TV, you make a better door than a window."

My wife is really immature. She talks all the way through *Transformers*. She'll just sit there and talk as if nothing's wrong. Meanwhile, you can't hear anything. All the dialogue is mud. I always have to turn around and say, "Do you mind?" Immature. Last week she threw away my army men. And get this. She didn't even ask. Immature.

Chapter Four

Enough from me. God bless you, and once again I can say that I was out here for ten minutes and nobody threw their panties at me.

Good night!

What He
Told Me

Let's begin somewhere. I don't know what "years" are,
so I guess I really couldn't tell you. Always remember
that there is only one sun in the sky and there is only
one of me. So don't bother me about what year it was.
It was any year I felt like. And you *will* bow and taste
hot steel. But only if I feel like it.

So don't bother me.

At any rate, we had just crushed the descendants of
the Scythians, and we were feeling pretty good about
ourselves. We were all out there on the plain, laughing,
messing around, slapping each other, stabbing. If you
want the truth, we were all about half bagged. We were
pouring whatever it was that the descendants of the
Scythians used to drink over *everybody*. We were just
cracking up.

It was a long time ago, but I still remember one particular descendant of a Scythian. His name was Dnargash

or something, one of those Scythian names. Anyway, this guy had the worst lisp I ever heard. I don't know about you, but if there's anything that really gets on my nerves, it's a lisp.

Anyway, this is a funny story. I'm riding along, nice day, not a care in the world. Suddenly I hear this guy behind me. He's talking just like this, I swear to God. I am not making this up.

NGASHO FLAM IK WEEDELL FURESY

Then he gets all excited:

IB FLUEW! NGASHO FLAM IK WEEDELL FURESY!

Right away I think, Cut me a break. Then I swing my horse around, bring my sword back, and his head is history. I didn't even watch the head, but I hear it went a long way. Someone told me 500 feet, but I don't know. Numbers don't mean anything to me. By that I mean numbers don't mean *anything* to me.

All I know is that I made a full, smooth swing, and I made contact. All spring I had worked on cutting down on my swing and just *meeting* the head. I had tried to stop trying to *kill* every head I saw up there.

It had paid off. It was the best year I ever had as a barbarian. I had learned patience. I was a little more mature now, and I had learned to wait on a head.

I enjoyed a great success. On top of everything else, we won the Eastern Roman Empire, which was the icing on the cake. I only wished my father could have been there to see it all, but then I remembered I had killed him a long time ago.

I slept well that winter. I had earned it.

.   .   .

I loved all my teammates when I was a Hun, but I guess I was closest to Thornells and Oenfig. We were an unlikely trio. Thornells's mom was one of the Kirghiz, and he talked about her often, but Oenfig's mother had been dismembered by the Kirghiz. Those two guys were as different as night and day. Me? Where did I fit in? I wouldn't know a Kirghiz from a Hungarian.

Still, the three of us hit it off almost right away. We were inseparable until Thornells got pole-axed and Oenfig got traded. I could tell a lot of stories about us three, but it's hard to think of one that you could tell in mixed company!

We were young then.

There's this one I can tell.

We had just slaughtered a lot of Teutons, I think it was. Omran, who was "one as the sun is one" at that time, told us all to take a break but be sure not to go anywhere.

That was all we needed.

We were not above bending the rules in those days, as is well known. We waited until Omran turned around. Then we hightailed it out of there and headed for the nearest town, which was some ways off. It was late, but we thought we might find an after-hours place.

We rode hard. Our horses were foaming and so was Oenfig, if I remember right.

We finally got there only to find that not only were there no private clubs, the whole place was dry!

We rode back frantically, cursing everything we could think of. It was very late and the one thing we didn't need was another fine.

We rode until we could see the campfires. Then we

walked our horses up and blended into the crowd. It looked like we'd made it.

Then I heard it. That voice. I knew it instantly.

The jig was up.

It was Omran. He didn't seem real happy about our little field trip.

"Attila! I'm glad you could make it. We're not busy or anything here, so I'm glad you could find it in your schedule to drop by."

I felt like digging a hole and crawling in it, but I had tried that before. Now I knew that digging a hole and crawling into it would make Omran even crankier than he already was. And he was plenty cranky, thank you very much.

"I see you and that bum Oenfig have been gone for, oh, some long period of time."

Even though Omran was the "one as the sun is one" at that time, he was not real good with numbers. He was not a stupid man, though. He was like a lot of us back then. Born before the Depression.

Anyway, Oenfig and me were temporarily "unclean ones." We would have to ride in the back. All the way in the back. Behind the rookies, even. We would be called, by everyone, "Namd-Kark," or "without foreskin."

We looked over at Thornells and he was just smiling to himself and whistling. Like it was Sunday in the park.

Thornells, Oenfig, and me, we had a lot of laughs together. We were boys then.

When people ask me about Omran I have only one thing to say: I loved the man. We had our share of differences,

116

but I can tell you: he was always tough but he was always fair.

Whatever else you can say about him, and it's probably plenty, he was one of a kind.

He had a very colorful way of talking. After a while we got to calling the things that he said "Omranisms." He was full of these things. Every time he opened his mouth you were liable to hear one.

"The Steppe-Land? Nobody goes there anymore. We slaughtered everyone and took their possessions. We made the strong ones slaves."

"It's not over until we have massive carnage."

"If people don't want their cities looted and burned, there's no way you're going to make them."

Whatever else he was, and it's probably plenty, he was one of a kind.

Of course one day I looked over at Omran, and he looked a little old. So I killed him.

A lot of kids ask me questions, but I guess the question I get asked the most is, "What does it take to become the leader of a vast horde of bloodthirsty, pitiless barbarians?" I always tell them the same thing: desire. You can have everything else: shortness, ugliness, a violent disposition, semi-insanity—it doesn't matter if you don't have that thing called desire. Without that, you'll never make it as a Hun. There are plenty of other things you can be. There are a lot of short, violent doctors, for instance. It's a big world and there aren't that many barbarian hordes. Find your niche and stay there.

If you think you have what it takes, leading a horde

of murderous troublemakers can be one of the most rewarding lives you can have.

Just what makes a Hun? Let's see.

Mental outlook is important, but you can't overlook the physical side. You have to be in tip-top condition if you plan to spend all your spare time swarming over the plains of eastern Europe. We have a long season, and staying in shape is a number one priority. Eat right and get plenty of rest.

Go down this list and see if you measure up.

1. You have to have a strong desire to learn the toughest job there is.
2. You have to take a real sincere pleasure in mayhem and carnage.
3. You can't be squeamish.
4. You should have a good throwing arm.
5. You can't be afraid of horses.

If you measure up, you may be Hun material. Maybe. Remember, again, there are lots of jobs around and not everybody can be a Hun leader. If everybody was a Hun leader, things would be a lot different, believe me.

In closing, let me say that Hun is not an easy position. But we do have protective equipment. Remember that, and never be afraid to use it.

Chitown Fans
Bid Farewell
to Hef

"For Hugh Hefner, the party is clearly over."
—*Newsweek,* August 4, 1986

Let us now praise famous men, as an earlier sports pundit wrote, and it's as true as it was when he wrote it. The shadows are lengthening now. The days dwindle down to a precious few.

His leaves are turning.

His records are Homeric. Perhaps we will never see his like again. One thing is certain: we will never see his like in bathrobe and pajamas again.

He was not like other men. (All right, he might have been like other men in some ways, but as a general rule he was not like other men.) Men looked down at their shoes in his presence. Women got all excited and often had to be calmed down. He inspired hate and love. He was the king, but time humbles us all. In this ball game they call life, time is the big umpire. When time tells you to head back to the dugout, the dugout is where you head. The big umpire we call time makes no exceptions for kings.

That's why the party is over. Over for the Majordomo of the Mangos. Over for the Lord of the Loblollies. Over for the Cicerone of the Chihuahuas.

Turn out the lights now. Blow out your candle, Eliza. Time to hang 'em up.

He carried the whole thing to a higher level. A level where no mortal man had gone before. A level where the shock waves to the body twist and turn a man, and a man must learn to transmute those shocks into something greater than himself if he is to survive. At that level a man has to modify, curve, roll, warp, distort, groan, call his lawyer, beg. A man has to learn that there are no promises, no guarantees, no cheery postcards from home. No big hugs and a "How are you, sweetie."

Not at this level.

But now it's time to say good-bye. Good-bye to the Emperor of the Eclairs. Good-bye to the Czar of the Zeppelins. Good-bye to the Head of the Hefties.

Although the party is over, don't turn off all the lights. Not all of them. We have our memories. And we still have the man. Here in front of us at Wrigley Field. You would never know it to look at the man, but today has not gone well. It was a bad morning at the mansion. There were three flies spotted inside. No one seemed to be able to explain just how they got there. Last night someone chilled a bottle of Chianti by mistake.

It has been a rough time, a killing time. Yet he is above it all. As always, he is operating on a higher plane.

The Chief of the Congas. The Bwana of the Bonbons. The Director of the Dumplings. The Boss of the Buttons.

He has always had the ability to rise above the crowd, to occupy his own lofty perch. One of his strengths was his absolute certainty that he could put up with *anything*. And put up with it he did:

- Static electricity buildup on the Dhurri rugs
- Ed Meese's frequent phone calls
- Fluctuations in the price of bulk Pepsi
- LeRoy Neiman's prints all over the place
- LeRoy Neiman

Now he approaches the microphone and the hush of the crowd is almost palpable. He clears his throat and the echo of his cough reverberates through the vast, silent arena.

"Thirty-odd years ago a skinny kid with a dream and a pipe came here. His dream was simple. He wanted to live in a vast palatial estate surrounded by beautiful women. He also wanted to have a love grotto, and he never wanted to wear anything but pajamas and a robe. This skinny kid wanted to drink a lot of Pepsi, eat fresh popcorn, write about his philosophy, and watch first-run movies in his living room.

"I was that skinny kid. That kid with a pipe and a dream, but not a pipe dream. It wasn't a pipe dream, because that skinny kid's dream came true.

"Now, some people may say that I got a bad break. They might say that I got a bad break because the party's over for me. But I can stand here today and tell you

YO, POE

that as far as I'm concerned I'm the luckiest guy on the face of the earth."

He turns and he leaves, his final echo buried in the tumultuous applause.

It is exit time, Master of Muchachas.

It is *finis,* Executive of the Earmuffs.

The curtain has fallen, Big Cheese of the Caboodles.

It's time to call it a day, Floorwalker of the Flapjacks.

Good-bye, Pharoah of Foglights.

Adios, Honcho of Handwarmers.

Catch ya later.

My New
Season

I'd been slipping for a long time, but last season was my best. Nevertheless, this season we're going with a whole new look and a whole new approach. We had a great success with me last year, but we're not going to play it safe and stick with the same old formula. This year's me will be last year's me, only more now, more today.

Last year, as you recall, we concentrated a lot on white socks. White socks almost became the statement last year. This year we're moving into a lot of new areas: argyle, over-the-calf tan, dark brown, even yellow wool. Toward the middle of next season I'll be seen wearing nothing but black socks for three straight weeks. We'll have to see how the mail goes on that one; we're flexible, and we can admit when we make a mistake.

Then there's my teeth. Last year, we concentrated almost exclusively on the molars, which worked great. After a while, though, you'd go out to a shopping mall and you'd see dozens of suburban clones doing the same molar thing. It's gotten stale, so this year you'll see me dividing my time about fifty-fifty between the canines and the bicuspids. We are going to do a whole hour on my wisdom teeth later on in the season. A whole hour of wisdom teeth was a hard idea to sell, but we finally got everybody to go along with it. Risk-taking comes with the turf at this level.

This year I'm going to have a real Toyota. Last year a lot of people thought that what I was driving was a Toyota, but it was really a Datsun with the nameplate worn off. This year it's a real Toyota that I'll be driving in the action scenes, and I'm excited about that. When I drive up to the grocery store to get beer or dog food, you'll see me behind the wheel of a real Toyota. It's part of my contract this year.

My hair is going to be completely different this year. I'm staying with the same team that handled my hair last year—Burell's Family Hair Parlor—but this year we've arranged for Bud Burell himself to do the actual cutting. This will give me a whole new look. Bud has personally assured me that he's going to be really careful shaving off the little hairs on the back of my neck. Also, I have it in writing that nobody's going to nick me back there, so this year you won't be seeing any dried blood on my neck, like last year. I think we overdid it with the dried blood on the neck last year.

My sound track? Good question. I can't pretend that it's not important. Last year it was all National Public Radio and Berlitz Basic French tapes. That worked fine, but this year I'll be leaning toward whirring attic fans and corduroy pants that make a brushing noise when I walk. Once in a while I'll whistle, but I'm not going to whistle every week, the way I did last year. This year when I whistle it will be special. I'm going to do a two-hour thing at the beginning of the season, and I'll be whistling in that, but then I won't whistle again until late November, at the earliest. This year whistling won't be the norm—it will be an event. I think that's the way it should be.

Colors have always been important to my success, and they still are. This year I want everything to just *vibrate* with contrast! I want a red ketchup bottle on my metallic-mauve refrigerator door. I want a cheap oscillating fan with transparent blue blades right in front of a stark-white dishwasher. I have this vision of a dark-brown wooden bookcase in front of a wall *covered* with flowered wallpaper. My colors have to be wildly juxtaposed if the whole thing is going to work. This year we're staying with colors, just like last year. The only difference is that we're going to use different colors, is all.

We know which side my bread is buttered on. My success came from being hip and high-style, but it was my *attitude* that was really the big factor, and I'm not messing around with that. My attitude is going to be exactly the same this year. Nobody has to worry about that. I'm still going to be hip. And I'm still going to be high-style.

Let me talk about something a little bit more sensitive here, if I might. I have been accused, by people who should know, of being too hip for my own good. Some of these people have said that last year a lot of my dialogue went right past them. It was gone almost before folks even had a chance to hear it and respond. Also, some people said that my whole life was really just a rock-video montage, without any substance behind it. I've listened to these complaints and criticisms, and while I don't agree with them I am going to do something about them. This year I'm going to go out of my way to show myself as a real three-dimensional person. You'll see this when my parents are featured for an hour, later in the year (around January), and I'm seen as having a real part in the relationship, with real emotions and real feelings. I was very emphatic about this when we prepared for the new season. I don't want to become some trendy image. I want to be a real flesh-and-blood character that people can relate to.

My demos were, quite frankly, unbelievable last year. This year we're looking for more of the same. Eventually I can see me evolving into a very hip, very modern continuation of some of the people who were here before me. But all that's in the future—so far in the future that it's hard for me to get a focus on it yet. Right now, I've got this new season in front of me, and that's enough.